PUPPETS OF PRAGUE

David Canford

MAD-Books.com

This novel is a work of fiction and a product of the author's imagination. Any resemblance to anyone living or dead (save for named historical figures) or any entity or legal person is purely coincidental and unintended.

Cover Design By: Mary Ann Dujardin

Cover photo: Anita Jankovic

Sign up at DavidCanford.com to receive David Canford's email newsletter including information on new book releases and promotions and claim your free ebook.

CHAPTER 1

The euphonic chiming bells of Prague's churches awakened him. Stefan rubbed his eyes, stretched his arms above his head and smiled as his consciousness grew.

It was a sound which had been part of his life since birth. When reminiscing, his mother would recount how as a baby he bawled often but would stop immediately the bells began to ring, his eyes darting around the room before a wide grin would appear on his face.

Getting out of bed, Stefan flung open the window to welcome the weak rays of February sunlight and let in Sunday. It was the best day of the week, the one day when he didn't have to work in his father's workshop.

Their location in a back street on the hill leading up towards the castle afforded Stefan a magnificent view over the russet rooftops of Mala Strana interspersed with church domes, and beyond them rose Petrin Hill, its slopes bedecked in frost and its trees skeletal in the absence of leaves. The sapphire sky above spoke of cold but of promise too, a glorious day to come.

"Stop daydreaming and get dressed or we'll be late," his mother scolded him as she flung open the door to his room.

After a hastily downed coffee, Stefan accompanied his parents down the steep, cobbled street towards St Nicholas, the bells in its light green copper-roofed belfry calling the faithful as they had for two hundred years. The church was a baroque masterpiece redolent of Italy, a piece of the Mediterranean here in Bohemia.

His mother clung tightly to her husband's arm, worried about tripping. She wore her best clothes as she always did when attending church and that caused her to be rigid in her gait. A rip or a tear in her long dress which swept the ground was what she feared most. She wouldn't relax until they were home again and she could hang it up in the wardrobe like a museum piece, safe from mishap. Save for the obvious difference in age, Stefan and his father looked almost identical in their black suits and black hats.

The family ascended the front steps of the colossal building, abandoning the bright sunshine for a dim and hushed world. Here Mozart had once played the organ. But despite its extravagant interior of soaring columns and frescoes and gold, Stefan considered time spent here as something to be endured. A penance to be paid until he was released into the beckoning freedom calling to him from outside throughout the service, a buzzing in his ear to hurry.

Once church had finished, he raced home to put on his everyday attire. Woe betide him if he should damage his suit or get dirt on it. Although he was almost eighteen, his mother's agility with a broom handle remained undiminished, and in their small apartment there was no chance of escape.

The remainder of the day was his to do as he wished. On Sundays, he got to enjoy his beautiful city, come rain or shine. Equidistant between the Baltic and the Mediterranean, she was Central Europe personified, her winters harsh, her summers scorching. A place ripe for invasion as warring armies had ebbed and flowed across this land. The Czechs had been obliged to live under the domination of others for centuries, currently as part of the Austro-Hungarian Empire. Yet out of conflict had arisen this architectural jewel and the inhabitants, against all the odds, had succeeded in preserving their culture.

But such matters were of no concern to Stefan when, after what had seemed an interminable mass, he hurried skates in hand to the Vltava river which dissects the city and where his friends would be waiting.

It had been several summers ago when the three of them had first met, each arriving at the river for a swim to cool off. The oven which the sun often became at that time of year roasted those inhabitants who chose not to take a dip until they were forced to retreat to the dark corners of their homes to seek respite and long for the cooler days of autumn.

Both Stefan and Matous had run to Rudi's aid when an aggressive swan broke from his group, his long neck up and wings flapping. He ran towards Rudi, the bird's feet barely breaking the surface of the water. The breeze from the swan's wings would have been welcome had Rudi not been terrified. He stumbled backwards in the shallows, falling on his backside. The other two ran between, screaming maniacally at the creature which skidded to a halt before settling down onto the water and silently gliding away to preserve his dignity in the face of uneven odds.

"Thanks you two. That was a close call." He stood up and offered his hand. "I'm Rudi."

"Stefan."

"I'm Matous. Are you still up for a swim?"

Rudi nodded. They spent the next hour swimming in and out of the shadows cast by the blackened statues of saints standing along the length of Charles Bridge, which links Mala Strana, the so-called Lesser Town, with Stare Mesto, the Old Town, and enjoying water fights close to the shore.

Similar in appearance in many ways, each boy had hazel eyes and brown hair, though Rudi's hair was the lightest and Matous' the darkest. And in height they ranged from Stefan who was fairly short to Matous the tallest, a reflection of their family's wealth or lack of and the nutrition they each received. Rudi had a face which was quite angular, the other two ones which were more spherical.

"Are you hungry?" asked Matous as they lounged by the water's edge afterwards, drying quickly in the hot air without need of a towel.

"Always," answered Stefan.

"Let's go back to my place then. It's only a few minutes from here. Cook will give us cake."

"Cook? What does your father do if you can afford a cook?"

"Something in finance, I don't really understand what."

Matous led them towards Charles Bridge and under it, and then across a small bridge over Devil's stream that makes Kampa an island but only just. A stone carving of a wolf adorned the top of the substantial front door into Matous' family home. In a kitchen as large as Stefan's parents' entire attic apartment, the youths demolished the plateful of makovy kolacek, small round brioches filled with jam and topped with poppy seeds, which the cook had laid before them.

"And what does your father do, Stefan?" asked Matous between mouthfuls.

"He makes puppets, like my family has always done. I will work with him when I'm older."

"I'm a huge fan of puppet shows, it's part of what makes this city what it is. And yours, Rudi?"

"Mine works printing a newspaper."

"Which one?"

"The Prager Tagblatt."

That a Jewish family lived in a luxurious dwelling on Kampa Island and not the ghetto raised no eyebrows. Renamed Josefov, in gratitude to Emperor Josef II, who had decreed religious tolerance, the requirement for Jews to live in the ghetto had been abolished over a hundred years earlier. On the city streets, both Czech and German were heard. Early twentieth century Prague lived in a large degree of harmony. Those of Czech, German and Jewish heritage could be friends.

That summer the three youths had bonded like the three musketeers, one for all and all for one. And forever it seemed.

CHAPTER 2

"What kept you so long?" demanded Rudi, stamping his feet and rubbing his hands together against the cold.

"What do you think? Count yourself lucky you weren't brought up a Catholic. Where's Matous?" asked Stefan as they sat down on a bench to put on their skates.

"Already out there on the ice, eyeing up the pretty girls."

Skating was not only great fun but a chance to admire the young beauties of Prague. They weren't to be found taking a dip in the Vltava in summer, after all swimming attire would not be considered lady like. In winter, bundled up against the cold in coats and fur hats, they could preserve their modesty.

The ice occasionally emitted a cracking sound as if it was complaining about being cut repeatedly by the sharp blades. But this didn't concern the teenagers, it always made that noise.

The young bucks had style. Backs bent slightly at the waist and hands clasped behind them, they moved fluidly and confidently, eyes prowling in search of young women to impress, rising to smile at them and coming to an abrupt stop whilst pirouetting around on one leg like a ballet dancer in the hope of eliciting a reciprocal smile or a shy giggle.

Stefan had spotted his quarry. He had passed her several times now, her black hair long and wavy, her cheeks rosy, and her lips divine. When he smiled at her, she lowered her gaze but he detected a coquettish acknowledgement. As he closed in on a return pass, he came to a halt.

"Good day, I'm Stefan," he announced with aplomb.

"Dagmar." Her response was almost inaudible.

"Are you here alone?"

"No, with friends. I must go."

She looked around but appeared unable to see them. Stefan and Dagmar had drifted some distance from where other skaters were. Without even a goodbye, Dagmar began skating towards the nearest part of the river bank. Disappointed, Stefan watched her go, becoming smaller on the huge canvass of the river.

Unexpectedly, she halted and made a series of jerking movements. One leg disappeared from under her and then the other. Stefan snapped out of his trance and began accelerating across the ice. Underneath his skates, the noise of cracking had become louder than normal. Undeterred, he continued to advance. Dagmar was by now almost fully immersed, grabbing at the ice breaking around her.

"Give me your hands," he cried.

Stefan was on his knees, reaching out to her. Her eyes were wide with terror and it was likely only seconds until she would go under. Heaving with all his might, he pulled her out. Silent with shock, she stumbled when she went to stand, water dripping from her.

"I've got you," he said as he held her up by the waist. "Let's get you back on dry land." He led her by the hand as she skated hesitantly, unnerved by each moan from the ice. "Where are your friends?"

"I can't see them," she shivered. "They must have gone."

"Where do you live?"

"Novy Svet."

Stefan wondered what to do. Novy Svet, or New World, was beyond the castle. She couldn't walk that far in her condition. Matous and Rudi arrived by their side and Stefan explained.

"Let's go to mine, it's the nearest," said Matous. "The fire's on and she can change into some of my sister's clothes."

When they arrived, the lads entrusted Dagmar to the care of Johanna, Matous' sister, and waited in the kitchen, nursing cups of hot coffee in their hands and enjoying the heat coming from the stove.

"I never knew the lengths you'd go to get a girl," teased Rudi.

"I'm just glad I was able to rescue her in time. I've not seen the ice crack like that before, not while skating's still allowed."

"Maybe it was that warm spell we had a week ago. It must have weakened the ice," said Matous. "I expect they'll prohibit skating on the Vltava for the rest of the season. Who knows when we'll all get to do it together again. I'm off to Paris come September to study the violin. Father says if I want to become a professional that's the best place."

"He's agreed to you not becoming a banker then?"

"Yes, Rudi, he's finally relented. Anyway what kind of banker would I make? I'm hopeless with figures."

Johanna entered the room.

"Is she all right?" asked Stefan, a distinct note of anxiety in his voice.

"She will be. We ought to get her home."

"I can escort her on the tram."

"A cab will be quicker, and it's a long walk from the nearest tram stop to her house. Matous will you go get one? I would accompany her but I have homework to finish. You should go with her, Stefan."

Dagmar was pale when she emerged from the drawing room with Johanna to be escorted to the horse and carriage waiting outside and could manage only a wan smile and half a wave as the others lined up to watch her depart.

"How are you feeling?" asked Stefan as he climbed in next to her.

"Not great yet. But thank you for what you did, it was brave."

Dagmar turned to look out of the window. Stefan accepted that as her way of saying she didn't want to talk. When they arrived on the narrow street in a hollow beneath the castle complex that was Novy Svet, he got down first and held out his hand for her to alight.

A woman appeared at the door, her frown pronounced.

"Dagmar, what's happened to you? And just what are you wearing, whose clothes are these?"

"The ice broke and she fell in the river," volunteered Stefan.

Her mother took in a sharp breath at the news. "And you're here because?" Her tone was more than a little acerbic.

"I was able to rescue her. We went to a friend's house to get her warm and for some dry clothes."

The woman's unfriendly demeanour softened slightly. "Well, thank you young man, we're forever in your debt. Let's get you inside and into bed, Dagmar. We don't want the neighbours talking." Her mother put her arm around her daughter and guided her inside.

"May I come in a few days to see that she's all right?"

Dagmar's mother's pinched expression, no doubt acquired from a lifetime of discontentment, intensified. "I suppose so," she said and shut the door firmly.

Stefan followed the steep alley up to Hradcanske Namesti, Castle Square, bordered by palaces and the entrance to the castle complex. Already smitten, his mind was whirling with the events of the day and excitement that he would be seeing Dagmar again.

Here above the city, those who ruled the Czech lands could live in splendid isolation. It was a place of silence compared to the urbanity below, disturbed only by horses' hooves or the synchronised marching at the changing of the guard. Atop the gates leading into the castle sat the Empire's coat of arms, a double-headed, crowned black eagle, resplendent with heraldic shields and decoration of gold and red and white. However, the eagle's hostile eyes, long red tongues and sharp claws told of aggression and an insatiable appetite for war.

CHAPTER 3

Stefan waited three days until he could suppress his desire to see her again no longer. Dagmar's mother was unwelcoming in her greeting.

"She is still weak. Wait here in the parlour." She opened the door to the room for him and made to go but then hesitated. "Tell me, what is it you do exactly?"

"I work in the family business."

"Which is?" the woman persisted.

"We make puppets."

"Puppets," she repeated the word, ending with a sniff of disapproval.

Stefan stood waiting. The room was gloomy and in deep shadow, opposite a high wall across the street. Located in a valley and facing north, little light found its way into Novy Svet at this time of year.

"A couple of minutes only," said mother to daughter as she ushered Dagmar into the room.

"How are you, Dagmar?"

"Much improved thank you. Mother is making such a fuss." Stefan shifted awkwardly from one foot to another. "Won't you sit?"

He sat on one of the two wooden chairs by the fireplace and Dagmar on the other. Like his own home, the furniture was functional rather than comfortable or desirable.

"I don't think your mother approves of me."

"I'm afraid not. She has delusions that I will marry a lawyer or a doctor."

"And you?"

"I don't even think about such things, I'm only seventeen."

Stefan could feel all momentum failing. If he said nothing that would be it, the opportunity gone. He had rehearsed many times on the walk here but now the words choked him and he had become uncomfortably hot.

"I was wondering…" His delivery was high pitched and he coughed to try and disguise it. "If…if you might like to take a walk sometime. On Petrin Hill, maybe."

"Mother wouldn't approve."

"Oh." He didn't resist and prepared to retreat.

"But I shan't tell her. How about next Sunday afternoon? We could meet outside the Strahov monastery."

Stefan smiled, a smile which was curtailed when Dagmar's mother burst in. Stefan leapt to his feet, feeling guilty about the concealment they had hatched and hoping it didn't show.

"We appreciate you coming but Dagmar needs to rest. However, you need worry about her no longer. She will recover completely in the fullness of time so there is no need for you to return. Let me show you out."

"Goodbye, Dagmar." Stefan gave a slight bow with his head. Once out in the street, Stefan ran several steps, propelled by sheer delight.

Sunday was a day of grey damp but Stefan was bathed in internal sunshine while he waited beneath the white washed facade and green onion domes of Strahov. Even higher than the castle complex, the view from here on a fine day was outstanding. Beneath the small vineyard in front of the monastery, the entire city stretched towards the hills on the horizon, spire upon spire, dome after dome. The iconic black pointed gothic steeples of Our Lady before Tyn in the Old Town, at once both sinister and like something from the pages of a fairy tale, shouted the loudest for the eye's attention.

Stefan's stomach churned when he saw Dagmar approaching. Her pallor was gone and the vitality which had enchanted him as he had circled her on the ice had returned. Dagmar's smile of hello was restrained but her eyes shone. In her hair, which was styled in a French plait, she wore a bright green bow. He thought her enchanting.

They took the pathway traversing the hill towards the summit of Petrin. Despite the bleakness of the low cloud cover, the chirping of birds in the trees was a reminder that spring wasn't far away.

"What did you tell your mother?"

"That I was meeting my friends. And you?" asked Dagmar.

"Mine's given up asking. She tells me I'm as uncommunicative as a statue. What about your father?"

"He's away in Vienna."

"That sounds very grand."

"Not really, he's a lowly government clerk. He usually goes there a few times a year. He says he only gets to go because his boss wants him to come along to take notes for him."

"Do you have brothers and sisters?"

"Not now, my brother died of measles. And you?"

"No, only me and my parents."

They had reached the top of the hill and the look-out tower which resembled a smaller version of the Eiffel Tower in Paris.

"Have you been up it?" asked Stefan.

"No."

"Me neither. I was going to suggest we did but given the weather I think perhaps we should come back in a few weeks time on a better day and when all the blossom is out."

Dagmar let out a laugh. "So you assumed I would agree to meet you again."

"I hoped so."

"Well, did you kiss her?" asked Rudi as the three friends wandered the streets of Mala Strana later in the day.

"That's private."

"You mean you didn't."

"Or perhaps it's because he's a gentleman," said Matous.

"Or a chicken," countered Rudi.

"Oh and you've kissed so many girls, I suppose," challenged Stefan.

"I will when I'm ready. I'm too busy with my apprenticeship right now."

His two friends laughed.

Stefan did kiss Dagmar on their third date. Her mouth was deliciously soft and his closeness to her fired a desire whose strength took him by surprise. Thoughts of her filled nearly his every waking hour. Even the daily grind of carving puppets became a thing of pleasure as his mind wandered, escaping the confines of the dusty workshop for imagined walks with Dagmar through the parks of Prague.

"You've ruined it," admonished his father when Stefan absent-mindedly carved off a chunk of wood from the face of a puppet he had almost completed. "You have your head in the clouds these days. What's going on?"

"Nothing."

"Well, be more careful. You're costing me money I don't have."

Stefan wanted to tell him that he was in love but Dagmar was insisting it was too soon to tell her parents, and if his own knew they would be pestering him to meet her which she would almost certainly be reluctant to do. Still, it bothered Stefan that his friends met up with him and Dagmar, and yet he kept it secret from his mother and father.

Spring 2014 turned to summer. Stefan's world held out the promise of a permanent summer. Meeting Dagmar had happened at exactly the right time. Soon Matous would be off to Paris, and Rudi, who was learning to set the printing press for newspapers, now worked at night so was too tired most of the time to see Stefan.

That the Archduke Franz Ferdinand and his wife had been shot in Sarajevo in late June barely registered with Stefan. They might have lived at Konipiste castle less than fifty kilometres from Prague, and the man may have been heir to the Hapsburg throne but Stefan didn't care. What had happened to them had no bearing on his life. He had all he wanted, Dagmar and Prague.

CHAPTER 4

"You look glum," commented Stefan when Matous arrived to join him for a drink.

"I'm not going to Paris any longer."

"Here, drink this beer I got for you, it'll make you feel better." Stefan handed him the glass of golden liquid resting on the upturned wooden barrel they were standing next to outside a bar. "Na zdravi."

"Na zdravi," repeated Matous without enthusiasm as they clinked glasses.

"Why aren't you going?"

"Don't you ever read a newspaper?" exclaimed Matous with irritation. "There's going to be a war. Austria declared war on Serbia because of the Archduke's assassination which riled Russia, and now Austria's declared war on Russia. Not to mention that Germany's jumped on the band wagon and declared war on France and Russia so Britain's declared war on Germany."

"Then let's thank our lucky stars that we're out of the way here in Prague while they beat the hell out of each other."

"That's where you're wrong, we're eighteen now

and we're liable to be called up."

"But it's not our fight. Why should we Czechs get sucked in?"

"Because we're the subjects of Emperor Franz Josef, mere puppets who have to do what he commands."

Suddenly the smooth beer no longer tasted so good to Stefan. His heartbeat accelerated and his chest tightened. "When?"

"Soon I expect."

The hill seemed steeper than normal as Stefan walked home. He had to wait to cross Nerudova while a detachment of cavalry trotted down the street from the castle. Once he had enjoyed the spectacle, the splash of bright colour they made in their pale blue jackets and red trousers. Today the effect was completely different, they seemed very much like the occupying army that they were, their black helmets with a gold motif and a spike on top a threat, a threat to his life and all his plans.

The knock the next morning was forceful and impatient.

"I'll go," said Stefan's mother as she got up from the breakfast table. Her figure obscured the caller but not his words.

"Does Stefan Janicek live here?" The voice was authoritarian, clearly one accustomed to giving commands.

"Yes."

"Here are his call up papers. He needs to be at Franz Josef Station tomorrow morning by eight. No shows will be regarded as cowards and dealt with accordingly."

Stefan heard his mother let out a poorly suppressed groan of horror. Her eyes were rheumy when she turned. She laid the papers on the table before him and reached for her son's hand, squeezing it tightly.

"I should get down to the workshop to help Tatka," said Stefan.

When Stefan gave him the news, his father's shoulders sagged more than a lifetime of standing over a workbench had caused.

"You should go see your friends today, not be stuck in here."

"Will you manage?"

"I'll have to from tomorrow so I may as well get used to it now." He placed a hand of love on his son's shoulder. "Go."

Stefan raced first to Rudi's apartment. While he ran he thought of Dagmar. They weren't due to meet until Sunday. He didn't know what to do, he could hardly go visit her at home.

Frau Vogel opened the door to her apartment and blocked it, her arms folded.

"He's sleeping after his nightshift."

"Has he-?"

"Yes, the papers have just been delivered."

"Mine too. When?"

"Tomorrow morning."

"Me as well."

Frau Vogel had never shown emotion in all the years Stefan had known her and he was taken aback when she hugged him. "Look after each other."

She too must have surprised herself as the hug was only momentary and she brushed her hands against her dark blue dress as if displeased by a show of vulnerability.

When Stefan reached Matous' house he could hear the sound of a violin drifting into the street. Johanna let him in. When Stefan entered the room Matous had his back towards him. Matous' right arm was moving with feeling as his bow coaxed melancholy music from the strings. Stefan stood listening, his friend was playing the second movement of Mendelssohn's violin concerto. It was as if the instrument was weeping. When Matous finally turned, two wet lines ran down his cheeks.

"You too?" asked Stefan. Matous nodded.

That night Stefan struggled to sleep. It was the last night for probably a long time, maybe forever, that he would spend in this room, the room in which he had spent every night of his life. Some said the war would be over by Christmas but he didn't see how they could possibly know. Above all, his thoughts were consumed by Dagmar. He could write a letter but didn't know what to write. Stefan wasn't good with words, especially the written variety.

Agitated, he got up and crept out of the apartment and made his way down the four flights of stairs and into the workshop. Fumbling in the dark, he lit a candle. The cosy light it cast and the familiar smell of sawdust soothed him.

Puppets in different stages of preparation sat on shelves. Some were little more than blocks of wood with only a face or the start of one, or a collection of unattached limbs. Others were finished and dressed in the intricate costumes which his mother made. There was a king with long white hair and a beard, his queen in a dress of green and gold, a ballerina, a skeleton, and a jester in red. That character was Stefan's favourite and was normally used to introduce a performance.

In this light, their large eyes looked almost real as if they lived in a parallel world which no human could see. A place where they could move freely and without strings.

Stefan thought of visits as a young child to the puppet theatre in the Old Town, of how the devils and witches would scare him and he would bury his head in his mother's arms. Days which in retrospect were safe and comforting. The turning of the door handle made him start and his father shuffled in.

"I thought I might find you here."

The man's eyes were weary, dark half moons beneath them. His eyesight was poor after spending so much time struggling to focus on his wooden creations. Without his son to help, Stefan worried what would happen when his father could no longer see well enough to continue. Already his father's hands were covered in cuts from misjudgments with his carving tools. Stefan hoped the army would pay him regularly so that he could send the money home to his parents. But if Stefan was killed, what then? He shuddered at the thought.

"I was thinking how much I'm going to miss this place, and miss you and Mamka."

"We will miss you too but each day you are gone will be one day nearer to your return."

"I don't understand why we need to involve ourselves in their beastly war."

"Because we are not free to make our own decisions but maybe we won't have to do so ever again. Tomas Masaryk, you must have heard of him, is leading a movement for an independent homeland. If the Empire loses, that goal could be achieved sooner than we ever thought possible. We have already come along way. When I was your age, German was the official language, now it is Czech. Little by little, the tide of history is turning in our direction. Puppets like these that we make saved our mother tongue. When we first fell under Hapsburg rule in the seventeenth century, our invaders prohibited the use of Czech, and our ancestors were forced to speak German. It was only at puppet shows that Czech

was permitted. They were our only way of preserving our heritage."

"I know, you've told me many times."

"Well, it is something that bears repetition and
is worth remembering. It is the reason our
language didn't die. Without it, our culture
wouldn't have survived."

Stefan decided he couldn't leave home without
revealing his secret.

"Tatka, there is something you should know. I'm
in love."

His father grinned. "I was right then. I told your
mother that must be what had gotten into you.
Who is she, and why haven't we met her?"

"Her name is Dagmar, she lives in Novy Svet. Her
parents wouldn't approve of me so we've told no
one."

"Novy Svet. Her family are hardly aristocracy if
they live there. Does she know you're leaving?"

"No, I thought I would write."

"Write? No, you must tell her in person."

"But it's the middle of the night."

"So? You must find a way. If you don't, you may
regret it. Anyway, I'll leave you in peace. Good-
night, son."

Though there were more than two hundred steps
up to the castle, Stefan leapt up them two by two
and kept on running when he reached the top
until a stitch in his stomach forced him to slow.
Still panting, he reached her house. The lane beneath the back of the castle was dark, lit only

26

by the stars. Running his hand along the ground by the wall opposite, he found some pebbles and threw one up at the window, ready to run if the front bedroom should prove to be that of her parents. He had to throw a few of the small stones until the window opened. Fortunately, it was the outline of Dagmar which appeared.

"It's me Stefan," he called softly.

"What on earth are you doing here?"

"I've been called up, I'm going tomorrow morning. Can you come down? I wanted to say goodbye."

"Give me a moment."

A minute later she emerged in a long white nightdress and a woollen shawl which she held tightly around her shoulders.

"Dagmar, will you wait for me?" Impulsively Stefan sank to one knee, taking both her hands in his. They were so delicate and smooth, unlike his own, calloused and roughened from his labour. "Will you marry me when I get back?"

In the darkness, it was difficult to gauge her reaction. When she didn't respond immediately, Stefan's heart rate doubled.

"I...I don't know what to say. This is so unexpected, everything's happening so fast. Can I think about it?"

Stefan was glad the shadows hid his disappointment. He let go of her hands and stood up. "Yes, of course. I'll write to you. You'd better go inside."

"Take good care of yourself." She stood on her tip

toes and gave him a quick kiss on the lips, one that felt ambiguous in sentiment. Stefan moved back, his earlier exhilaration had turned to a vague feeling of resentment.

He made his way home, his legs heavy and slow. Damn this war, and damn the Hapsburgs and their empire. He and all Czechs deserved to be free, not to have their fate determined by foreigners.

CHAPTER 5

His parents' farewell had been tight hugs, quivering smiles and eyes which were fighting to stay dry until after he had descended the stairs. Neither Stefan nor Matous talked as they made their way together over Charles Bridge and wended their way through the cobbled side streets to Wenceslas Square and on towards the station. Each step was solemn as if they were following a funeral cortege and passing through their city for one last time. Matous carried his violin case, Stefan nothing. In his jacket pocket were a few folded sheets of paper and envelopes for letters home and a pencil to write with. The call up papers had told them to bring no luggage.

Like a magnet, the station drew hundreds of young men from all directions towards its art nouveau frontage, a final glimpse of beauty before they would enter into a cavernous interior of glass canopies proclaiming imperial power and funnelling them towards waiting trains.

"Hey, Rudi!" Matous had spotted their friend only a few paces in front. "I'm so glad we saw you. We can travel together and hopefully stay together."

It was another voice which caught Stefan's attention, a woman's voice. He halted and looked over his shoulder. Pushing through the crowd, she reached him.

"I'm so pleased I caught you." Her words were breathless.

"Dagmar," he smiled, the sorrow of separation forgotten.

"I'll wait for your return." She flung her arms around him, and they kissed to claps and cheers from those nearby. Stefan didn't want to ever let go but they didn't have the gift of time.

Matous tapped him on the shoulder. "We need to go."

"I'll write," promised Stefan as he backed away slowly, holding her hands with outstretched arms until he had to let them drop, reluctant to end that last touch, that last connection with home. Dagmar stood smiling through her tears, but newcomers abruptly came between them and she disappeared from view as if her presence had only been imagined. However, Stefan was renewed, he had more reason than ever to make it back now.

When they got on the train there was standing room only yet it was of no great consequence, the journey lasted but a few hours. Ordered to disembark, they were led to a decaying old castle which was to serve as their barracks. In a long line, it was some time until the friends reached the front. After a rudimentary medical, they were moved to another room to hand over their clothes in exchange for the light grey uniforms which eliminated their individuality and confirmed the awful reality of their situation.

That night, in his bed amongst the rows of sleeping conscripts, Stefan thought of this morning and the unexpected surprise. She had said she would wait. How wonderful was that. But then doubt began to gnaw at him. Did that mean her answer was yes, that she would marry him or was that to be determined on his return? He turned over and put his hands on his ears in an effort to block out the snoring all around him. The stale fug of so many crammed together he couldn't avoid. How his small room overlooking Mala Strana seemed like a palace now.

The next few days were ones of drills and charging at stuffed sacks with bayonets on the end of their rifles. Days of angry shouts from those commanding them, days without joy or hope.

"I can't imagine actually being able to kill anyone," said Stefan while he sat with his two friends on the hard baked earth of the castle courtyard one evening. The sun dipped out of sight, projecting the long shadow of the turreted wall over them as though an omen of the shroud of war which awaited them.

Rudi had no doubts. "It's them or us. If you want to see Dagmar again, it's the price you must pay. We won't survive if we worry about having to kill enemy soldiers."

"The Russians aren't our enemy. We're being asked to murder our fellow Slavs to uphold a regime that denies us our freedom."

"I'm not a Slav," protested Rudi. "The Emperor's given you back your language. When will you ever be satisfied? Only when you drive all the Germans out of Prague even though we too have lived in the city for hundreds of years and have as every much right as you to live there?"

"Independence wouldn't mean that, there's no reason why we can't all live in harmony," interjected Matous.

"Oh, so you think the same." Rudi's face reddened. "You should both be careful what you say if you don't want to be labelled traitors." Still simmering, he got up and walked off.

The following day, they were marched back to the train and taken closer to the front. Some distance short of it the railway ended in a small town. Their column was more than a kilometre in length, like a trail of ants along the rutted mud track climbing the hills in front of them. Horses hauled cannons and created a cloud of dust. Behind them donkeys pulled carts loaded with supplies. They brayed in protest when their drivers whipped them for stopping. From somewhere up ahead came a sporadic thudding like distant thunder. When they crested the hill tops, the land lay before them flat and featureless.

That night the army set up camp still short of the front. While night approached from the East obliterating dusk as though a silent invader, the three friends sat on the grass eating dinner out of their metal mess tins. Hungry and tired, they spoke little but something more than fatigue and hunger had subdued them. There was an awkwardness between them which had never existed before, accentuated by tension that tomorrow they would face battle for the first time.

"I'm going to turn in," said Rudi. He wandered towards the tents set up in long rows. Stefan and Matous remained, neither was keen to retire and allow the arrival of morning to be hastened by sleep. Most of the other men must have felt the same way as few went to bed.

Matous disappeared briefly, returning with his violin. He began playing a Czech folk tune. Soon many were on their feet, relishing this precious link with home as they danced. Each time Matous stopped, pleas for more echoed around him until finally he announced that he could play no longer. All stayed, talking quietly as they lounged on the grass while owls hooted in the night air and searched for food.

A couple of men came over and sat down next to Matous and Stefan, their facial features indistinct in the dark indigo of night, their voices earnest.

"A lot of us have been talking about tomorrow," said one. "We're Czechs not Austrians, wouldn't you agree?" Stefan and Matous nodded their assent. "There's a plan to surrender en masse. We should be helping Russia, not fighting her. She can help us get our freedom back, the freedom the Hapsburgs stole from us hundreds of years ago at the Battle of White Mountain. What do you say?"

"Count me in," answered Stefan without hesitation. "Matous?"

"My violin. I can't take it into battle. If I surrender I will never get it back."

"Nor can you play it if you're dead."

"All right, I suppose so."

"Good," said the colleague of the man who had raised the idea of capitulation. "The plan is simple. As we advance, we drop our weapons and raise our hands and let the Russians finish off any of our commanders who don't surrender."

"We should tell Rudi," said Matous after the two plotters had moved on.

"No," said Stefan. "He might warn the officers. He'll be able to make his choice when he sees what's happening."

"But if he chooses to fight, he'll probably be killed."

"In that case, we'll have to make sure he doesn't get the chance."

In the darkness, Matous' fingers explored the contours of his violin. He wondered if he would ever get to play it again as he moved his hand back and forth across the smooth, varnished wood, caressing the instrument like it was the lover who he had never known and might never live long enough to meet.

CHAPTER 6

Many slept outside that night. It was the chill of a dawn that they all worried might be their last which awoke the soldiers. The sky was streaked blood red, and dew had made their uniforms damp and their limbs stiff after a night spent lying on the ground.

As the sun rose, they were commanded to advance. A wide and moving wall of men. Out there but getting ever closer was another line of men, the huge imperial flag of the Tsar fluttering behind them. The sun climbed above it, a ball of white fire so bright that the Czechs could barely see any longer what they were heading towards.

The three friends marched side by side, rifles out in front of them, bayonets fixed, expressions grim. Stefan gripped his rifle tighter, hoping his friends wouldn't notice it move in his shaking hands. But they were too absorbed in their own worlds of fear, sweating profusely even though the air remained cool at this early hour.

"Charge!" An officer bellowed.

The men began a slow run towards the enemy but without conviction and without the aggression needed to survive.

"Now!" A soldier near them shouted, throwing his rifle to the ground and continuing forwards with raised hands. Up and down the line others copied him, including Stefan and Matous. Rudi looked about him, bewildered.

"What's going on? Are you all cowards?"

"We're surrendering. Drop your rifle, Rudi. Drop it or they'll shoot you," urged Matous.

"Never." He ran out in front, intent on fighting. Stefan chased after him and ploughed into him forcefully, pushing him over. Matous grabbed Rudi's rifle and threw it behind them. When he got up, Rudi was scowling.

"You'll thank us one day," said Matous but the disdain in Rudi's eyes was intense.

The Russian soldiers in front of them halted and cheered. They parted, allowing their soon to be prisoners to come through.

It was a long march to the prisoner of war camp. Rudi separated himself from the other two, preferring to walk with strangers than those he considered traitors.

"We did the right thing," commented Stefan. "He'll come round."

The camp, surrounded by forest, was large and sprawling. With an endless supply of wood all about, the prisoners were put to work to build their own huts and beds to sleep on. It wouldn't be a comfortable existence but they would have shelter when summer slipped south, and fires to huddle around when a new enemy, winter, arrived.

Rudi avoided his erstwhile friends. He joined the smaller group who hadn't wanted to surrender.

Stefan came across him one morning as he walked towards the latrine trench and Rudi was returning. Stefan halted.

"I'm sorry for pushing you like that, Rudi. But what was the sense in you getting killed, one against thousands?"

Rudi glared at him. "It wouldn't have been one against thousands if the rest of you hadn't betrayed those of us prepared to do our duty." He walked on, politics and war had driven a wedge between them.

Once the men had erected their accommodation, they were assigned work outside the camp, some working on farms to replace those away fighting, others to improve roads and railway lines for the transport of soldiers and supplies. Stefan and Matous were directed to a farm and given scythes to help with the harvest. For a young man used to sitting at a work bench carving puppets and another accustomed to playing the violin, it was back breaking work. It took what little energy they had left to haul their tired bodies back to camp each night where they collapsed on their beds. There were no mattresses, no pillows, and no bedding. They didn't care, within seconds of lying down on the hard wood, they were fast asleep.

At the end of one day, the man who had led the mass surrender, burst into their cabin to address the fifty or more who shared the cramped space.

"My fellow freedom fighters, I have a proposal. Some of you may have heard that there is a Legion fighting with the Russians consisting of Czechs and Slovaks who were already living in Russia before the war. Rather than wasting our time here, we should join them and help secure the liberation of our homeland. I'll be asking the camp commander to pass my proposal to his superiors. Are you with me?"

A loud affirmation confirmed that they were. A few days later news reached them that the Russians had refused, unprepared to trust those who had already deserted from one army.

Compounded by the heavy rains of autumn, the mood amongst the prisoners plummeted. As the front moved towards them, the camp had to be abandoned. They were marched further east where they had to begin the process of building huts to shelter in all over again. This time it was a race against the clock. The temperature was dropping daily, bringing first frost and then snow.

Prague seemed so very distant. Stefan wondered when he would ever return to his magnificent city and leave the overwhelming silence and emptiness of Russia behind. He still carried sheets of folded paper in his pocket on which he had written to Dagmar and his parents. But they remained in his pocket. There was no postal service, and even if there had been, he had no money for stamps. His parents must be worried, Dagmar too. Just how long would the war last and how long would she wait? Stefan worried too about how his parents were managing. His plans to send money home had been ruined in the mass surrender. As Christmas approached and the nights grew longer, the yearning for home became a constant in the pit of his stomach that rarely gave him peace.

Matous too missed home. On Christmas Eve, the two friends reminisced as they sat on the floor with their arms around their knees, squeezed next to others, all trying to stay close to the fire, their sole source of warmth and light.

"It was this time last year that I got to give a recital in the Rudolfinum. My family were so proud, a Jewish boy performing in Prague's foremost concert hall. I think seeing the reception I received there was a big factor in my father finally relenting and agreeing to me making music my career."

"I'll miss doing our annual Christmas puppet show for the children in the neighbourhood. My father and I always got such pleasure from seeing the joy on their little faces. Hey, do you remember it was usually right after Christmas that the Vltava froze and we could go skating."

"Ah, such happy times, the three of us." But a

frown appeared on Matous' face. "Did we do the right thing, Stefan?"

"Sometimes you have to make a choice for what you believe to be right. If, God willing, Russia wins and our country gets its freedom, Rudi will come to realise it's for the best because no longer will we be dragged into other people's wars, and then we can all be friends again."

"I don't want to wait that long. I'm going to find his hut and see how he's doing. He must be somewhere on the far side of the camp since we never run into him this end. Do you want to come along?"

In the second hut they enquired, they succeeded. "On that bed at the back, over there," a man told them. "Be careful, he's gone down with typhus."

CHAPTER 7

Rudi was tossing his head from side to side and mumbling incoherently. No one was attending to him and his breathing was stertorous. Matous and Stefan looked at each other and nodded. Matous removed Rudi's shirt, revealing the tell-tale rash on his body.

"I'll go get a bucket of water," volunteered Stefan. "We should try and get his temperature down."

They spent that Christmas by Rudi's side, sleeping on the floor by his bed like faithful canines, taking turns to clean up his vomit, cool him with a wet cloth on the forehead, and trying to make him comfortable. It seemed their efforts would be in vain. Rudi's condition showed no sign of improvement.

"It's not fair, he's too young to die," said Matous. "He hasn't lived, none of us have."

"Maybe we should pray," suggested Stefan.

Come the morning of the third day, Rudi was no longer delirious and sleeping somewhat peacefully. The two friends smiled through their exhaustion. He had been lucky, unlike many others in the camp who had already died from the disease. When he did open his eyes, his look was one of confusion.

"Why are you two here?"

"You've been very sick, Rudi. You're weak, you need to rest. We'll come back and see you tomorrow," said Matous.

The following day, Rudi was sitting up in his bed, his hair matted with the sweat from the last few days but in his face was some colour once more.

"How are you feeling?" asked Stefan."

"Much better than I was. Thank you for what you both did, the others here told me about it."

"You're our friend, Rudi, a dear friend," said Matous. "When you're up and about, why don't you move over to our hut?"

"I'm fine where I am thanks. We're all German speakers in here, and we understand how each other feels. I'll come over and see you in a few days. I'm tired now." Rudi slid down until he was lying flat and closed his eyes.

But Rudi never did come, and a couple of weeks later the prisoners' were told to get ready to leave, like nomads of the Steppes their camp was moving yet again. This time they were split into two groups. Their friend wasn't in theirs.

Monotony became ingrained in their daily lives. Nothing ever changed other than the seasons. News of the war was infrequent and inconclusive. At times it seemed as if their captivity might never end.

Over two years passed, two long years. To the young men, bored and frustrated that their best years were being wasted, it seemed longer. It was one morning in spring 1917 that Matous burst into the hut, his face animated, excited that he finally had something to report.

"I've just overheard the guards talking. The Tsar's been overthrown, Russia has a new government."

Stefan wasn't impressed. "How will that change anything for us?"

"I don't know. Still, if the Tsar can be overthrown, maybe the Emperor will be too."

But a new government in Russia brought no change to the lives of the prisoners of war. Buds opened on the silver birch trees, the temperature rose and mosquitoes began to bite.

It was in the dog days of summer while the prisoners lounged languidly outside on the dry, unyielding earth that three men in military uniforms which weren't Russian ones arrived in the compound. The prisoners sat up, curious to learn the purpose of their visit. One of the three stood on a wooden box and addressed them in Czech.

"My fellow countrymen," he began. "I'm an officer in the Czech Legion. As you probably know, the Russian government has been reluctant to let you prisoners fight. But thanks to the Legion's victory over the Austrians at the recent battle of Zborov, they are now willing to allow me to recruit you into the Legion to rejoin the war, this time on the side fighting to free our nation. Be under no illusions though, if you are captured the Empire will treat you not as prisoners but traitors and they will execute you. But if we win, our country could finally achieve its freedom. Who wants to join me?"

A collective roar of enthusiasm greeted his offer. The men got to their feet, smiling at each other and shaking hands at the welcome news. At last, their lives would no longer be meaningless. Within minutes, the prisoners were filing out of the camp, their once desultory demeanour replaced by a bound in their stride. Stefan's heart sung like it hadn't since before the war. They were out of the prison camp, able to make a difference. They had a goal. To create a country of their own.

Marched to the nearest base, they eagerly shed their now torn and tattered uniforms from the Austro-Hungarian army. After washing in the nearby river and shaving off their unruly beards, which had given them the appearance of deranged hermits rather than military men, they put on new uniforms of green, proud to be part of the army of their wished for new country.

Before long, they were back at the front. This time Stefan didn't experience the fear which had consumed him before. He was fighting for a cause in which he believed. He soon became accustomed to the sharp, slightly sweet smell of cordite, and explosions only metres away as he flung himself on the ground for protection. The first time he shot someone Stefan experienced remorse but not the second time or after that. It was as Rudi had said, kill or be killed.

The Legion now numbered in excess of forty thousand. Surely victory would be theirs, how could it not, thought Stefan and his comrades in arms The Czechs cemented their reputation for being tough and a difficult opponent to beat. The sclerotic Austro-Hungarian forces were no match for them. The Czechs seemed unstoppable.

It was one autumn evening while they were huddled around an outside fire warming themselves, mesmerised by the orange flames leaping upwards into the night that word reached them of a new and unexpected development.

"I've some bad news," said a soldier sitting down next to Stefan and Matous. "Lenin and his Bolsheviks have seized power and overthrown the new government. They say he wants peace at any price, that Russia will capitulate and give the Germans and Austrians vast swathes of territory to end the fighting."

"But we've got the enemy on the run," said Stefan. "It doesn't make sense."

"The Russians are deserting in droves and a civil war's breaking out. Lenin wants to focus on winning that."

"Where does that leave us?"

"Between a rock and a hard place, I'd say. Masaryk is apparently negotiating to get us passage to the western front so we can continue the fight from France."

"Hasn't anyone told him that Germany's between Russia and France?" said Matous. "Surely the Germans are going to demand our surrender. And if the Austrians get their hands on us, we already know that wouldn't go well. We could end up having to fight not just them but also the Russians."

Even the heat from the fire couldn't prevent at shiver running down his spine. They were trapped.

CHAPTER 8

That winter, energised by Russia's collapse, the German and the Austro-Hungarian forces went on the offensive pushing the Legion back. Just as the land had disappeared under snow drifts, all chance of escape and reaching France also disappeared. The high hopes of last summer had been blown away with the icy winds that never ceased in this desolate land. Then as the days lengthened and the intervals between battles were filled with the uplifting sounds of returning migratory birds, hope was rekindled.

"Masaryk has reached agreement with the Bolsheviks for us to have safe passage on the Trans Siberian to Vladivostok where the Allies will ship us out," announced their commander.

"I should probably have paid more attention in geography lessons at school, but isn't Vladivostok in the wrong direction?" Stefan said to Matous, like a ventriloquist barely moving his lips as the soldiers stood rigidly at attention.

"Yes, it's near Japan, about ten thousand kilometres east from here."

"Ten thousand," repeated Stefan in disbelief that

they could possibly get that far. "Maybe it's a ploy by Lenin to lull us into a false sense of security before he kills us all."

"I expect we're about to find out."

Fighting a rearguard action, the soldiers made it up to the railway line by the time the trees had thrown off their winter mourning and put back on their finest greenery. Soldiers from the Red Army watched the Czechs arrive. The silent stares of the Russians heightened the palpable state of tension in the air.

Stefan held the rifle hanging from his shoulder so tightly the whites of his knuckles showed. There were Russian soldiers on both sides of the column now. He wondered if the Legionnaires were but insects walking into the mouth of a Venus flytrap. Beads of sweat ran down from Stefan's forehead and dripped off his nose. Reluctantly, he and Matous followed others in throwing their rifles down under the watchful gaze of the Russian troops. The agreement Masaryk had made with Stalin, who at the time was a mere sidekick of Lenin, required the Legion to abandon most of its weapons.

They boarded a train which itself seemed to have no end like the track it would travel down. Yet even all those carriages weren't enough. Hundreds were left standing there, told another train would come but when nobody knew.

"Thank God we made it on," said Matous as they squeezed themselves onto a wooden bench seat, eliciting sour looks from those already on it. "I wouldn't want to be standing around waiting, not with those Bolsheviks. I don't trust them, not one bit."

"How long do you think the journey will take us?" asked Stefan.

"In normal times, a week, ten days maybe. But in times such as these, who can say."

Frequently the train stopped, halted by local Soviet militias who hadn't heard of the deal struck in Moscow. The explanations of the Legion's officers and the persuasive sight of so many soldiers, some of who remained armed, eventually resulted in free passage.

Out on the steppes the temperatures began to climb steadily.

"I can't believe we're going half way around the world to rejoin the war in France," said Matous. He and Stefan were sitting on the roof along with the many who chose to travel this way, preferring a warm breeze made hotter by the smoke from the engine to the claustrophobic interior.

"Indeed," agreed Stefan. "But you'll be handily placed to start at the Conservatoire in Paris when it's over."

"No, when it's over I want nothing more than to get back to Prague."

"Me too. I used to think once that I might want to travel, but being away from home makes you realise there's nowhere like it."

It took their train a week to travel only a few hundred kilometres to reach the city of Chelyabinsk. At this rate of progress, their journey was going last months. While their train passed slowly through the city, another came past from the opposite direction, men likewise crowded together on its roof.

"Look," pointed Stefan. "Austro-Hungarian prisoners of war. They must be freeing them and transporting them westward."

"Ouch!" The man next to Stefan cried out in pain as a stone hit his head.

"Filthy Czechs. Traitors!" came shouts from the men on the other train. Within seconds, men on both trains were leaping across the space between and pummelling each other.

Shots rang out.

"Stop that and get down here. Immediately, or I'll give the order to shoot."

Stefan let go of the Austrian who he had pinned down. On the platform stood a Red Army officer, his men lined up beside him and their rifles pointed upwards at Stefan and his colleagues. The Czechs complied.

"They started it," complained one as he got down.

"I'm not interested," responded the Russian commander. "Those men you attacked are under our protection."

"What are you going to do with us?" demanded

the man.

"Shoot you if my superior agrees. Now move it."
The men were marched at gun point into the
station building. "Sit down against that wall and
keep your hands on your heads, and don't move a
muscle."

In the oppressive stillness and humidity, a fly
landed on Stefan's nose. He blew upwards hoping to dislodge it but the fly merely moved to
his forehead. The Russians held their rifles out
towards the Czechs, keen it would seem from
their ghoulish grins to receive confirmation of
their orders. The clock on the wall ticked loudly,
a countdown to their execution. Captors and cap-
tives eyeballed each other. Stefan's uniform had
become damp with perspiration.

Their situation felt the most precarious which
Stefan had experienced despite months on the
battlefield. In the confusion and chaos of battle,
there was no time to think about dying. Here,
where nothing was moving and nothing happening, it seemed as if death was inevitable and
getting ever closer.

Without warning, the doors burst open. Legionnaires rushed in shooting the Russian guards before they had time to respond. Stefan leapt up,
shaken but relieved to see that all his colleagues,
including Matous, had survived.

"Take the rifles from these dead Russians,"
ordered the officer who had led the rescue. "It's
time to rearm every Legionnaire. We'll be fight-

ing our way to Vladivostok."

"Encountering those Austrian prisoners made me think of Rudi," said Matous to Stefan as he bent down over a dead body face down on the floor and took the rifle lying next to it. Months of fierce fighting had made them casual around the deceased. "Maybe he's been freed too and is with the Emperor's army and fighting on the Western Front. Wouldn't it be terrible if we faced each other in combat?"

"We are more likely to be struck by lightning. The way things are going, the war will be over before we ever get back to Europe, and Rudi will have got back to Prague long before us."

Soon the Legion had Chelyabinsk under its control. Enraged, Trotsky, in command of the Red Army, ordered the arrest and detention of all Czech and Slovak Legionnaires. Battle hardened, they fought back and before long had taken control of most of the Trans Siberian. It is even said that fearing the Czechs would move on to Ekaterinburg caused the Bolsheviks to assassinate the Tsar and his family to prevent the Czechs freeing them.

Stefan and Matous continued their slow journey eastwards. Ever resourceful, they and their colleagues adapted to a life on the rails. They fixed machine guns to carriage roofs and turned one wagon into a bakery and another a brewery to create the beer for which their home city was rightly famous. Matous deployed his artistic talents to help decorate the exteriors, on one creating an image of Prague castle, and on another a picture of a falling soldier and the words "Death is better than the life of a slave."

A band of brothers stretched across thousands of kilometres. They seemed invincible. Invincible until late one summer's evening under a herring bone sky of pink clouds, a behemoth lumbered down the track towards them. It looked unlike any train that they had ever seen. As it grew closer, its features came into focus. Wrapped in steel armour, bristling with machine guns and bookended by cannons that looked like massive tank turrets, it was the stuff of nightmares. Stefan and Matous, who were on duty manning machine guns on the roof, swallowed hard as their own train ground to a halt before this metal monster. No amount of patriotism and sheer grit could overcome this enemy.

CHAPTER 9

"It's ok lads," smiled the commander who was up on the roof with them and had been looking through his telescope. "It's one of ours, they're Legionnaires not Bolsheviks."

The men clambered down from the train and walked beside the rails to inspect the most powerful war machine any of them had set eyes upon.

"Where on earth did you get this beauty?" their commander called up to a man peering out of one of the turrets.

"We fought the Russkies for it in Simbirsk. They called it Lenin. We've renamed it Orlik, young eagle."

The soldiers admired Orlik, touching its metal casing as if to confirm that it was in fact real. An officer jumped down from a flatbed wagon and saluted their commander.

"I have orders for you and your troops. You are to proceed to Irkutsk and ensure continued control of the line for one hundred kilometres either side of the city."

"For how long? Until we have evacuated all our

troops?"

"The situation has changed. For the time being, we are staying. Our political leaders have agreed to a request from the Western Allies to maintain possession of the Trans Siberian railway to assist the White Army in its fight against the Reds. Masaryk believes it will garner support from the Americans for a new state combining Bohemia, Moravia and Slovakia to be known as Czechoslovakia with Prague as its capital."

"Finally," said Stefan to Matous, "our nation is almost a reality. What a thrill it would be not only to get home but to arrive back in a new country, our own country."

Their journey continued, the Trans Siberian passing through a barely interrupted forest like the walls of a fortress they were never able to see over. Apart from small settlements, which were few and far between and the very occasional town, they saw little but trees except where railway bridges crossed wide rivers and they could for a moment look towards the horizon. Progress remained frustratingly slow. Sections of track had been ripped up and some of the bridges damaged by the warring Russian factions.

It was already late summer when they got to within a hundred kilometres of Irkutsk. An officer entered the carriage where Mathew and Stefan were playing cards with other soldiers. They had long since abandoned looking out of the window, the view hardly ever altered and

DAVID CANFORD

was without interest for the most part.

"Right you lot, welcome to your new home. You are to guard this piece of track. You can billet yourselves with the locals. I'll have some supplies sent down the line from Irkutsk when we get there."

Stefan looked out of the window. Through the numerous specks of black dirt left from the engine's smoke, he could discern a one street village of perhaps twenty houses, all made of wood which had darkened with age and a few barns. The settlement started not far back from the track and ran northward a short way until surrendering to the all encroaching taiga.

"Well, what are you waiting for? Off you get. Now!" barked the officer.

Fifteen young men disembarked. They were met by a handful of curious faces, men with full beards, dressed in caps, tunics, and trousers of coarse material that looked to be no better than burlap, and a couple of women in black dresses and shawls which they promptly placed around their heads when the soldiers looked in their direction.

With a swoosh of steam, the train, which had been not only their home but their protection for the last few months, began to move. The men turned, watching it slip ever farther away and leaving them adrift in this land without pity.

In Russian, that the Legionnaires had picked up to varying degrees during their years in the country, Havel Smolek, the men's captain, addressed the villagers in his deep voice.

"We're your friends, here to protect you from the Red Army. We'll need food and shelter."

The locals appeared to be cowed by the sight of their rifles, but one man stepped forward, his arms folded. He was a bear of a man, toughened by a life of hardship.

"We don't want you here. If the Bolsheviks discover we're sheltering you, they'll slaughter us all."

"That's not going to happen. We and our colleagues are in control of Siberia."

"No one can control this land, it's too vast. And one day you'll leave and then what?" retorted the man.

"We'll only go when the White Army has won."

The man cleared his throat and spat on the ground. "They're no better than the Reds. We're Jews, both sides hate us. We came here when they drove us out of our homes in Ukraine and burned them down."

Havel's tone hardened. "You don't have a choice, we're not leaving. You either co-operate with us or you can leave and live in the forest."

"Well, you'll have to sleep in the barns with the animals. We're not having you in our homes sleeping under the same roof as our daughters."

"Winter's coming," said Smolek. "I'll not have my men sleeping in barns. If you're worried about your daughters then some of you need to move out of your homes and move in with others so we too can sleep in a place with a stove. And you'll need to feed us until supplies arrive. You'll be paid when the train bringing them comes."

"Hmm." The man stuck his chin out but understood his village had to bend like the trees in the wind. They had nowhere else to go and wouldn't survive a winter in the forest.

Allocated the two houses nearest the railway line, the soldiers set about settling in. It was the largest living space and the greatest comfort which they had enjoyed since leaving their homes in Prague. Come the evenings, it was a cosy refuge of wood smoke and ribaldry along with the assuring smells of hearty stews slowly cooking. There was a peace here the men hadn't expected to find.

A few days after their arrival, Matous went for a wander following a well worn path through the trees. It brought him to a wide river. At this time of year the water had fallen to its lowest level. A woman in a headscarf with her back to him was seated on the pebble beach.

"Hello."

Startled, she jumped to her feet and faced him. She wore a white blouse and plain brown skirt stopping just short of her scruffy black shoes. Young with almond shaped eyes of green and a pale skin lightly freckled she wasn't a classic beauty, but her face had a quality which held an observer's interest.

"I'm sorry, I didn't mean to frighten you. I'm Matous."

"Raisa."

"Nice to meet you, Raisa."

"I must be getting back. My family will be wondering where I am."

She hurried past him. Matous stayed, skimming stones on the river's surface, but his thoughts were elsewhere.

CHAPTER 10

Despite not being from a particularly religious family, Matous took to joining the village men in the synagogue and gained their trust. He didn't receive the sullen looks of resentment given to the other soldiers for having occupied their village and putting their families in danger.

Matous did his best to engineer opportunities to see Raisa whenever he could. Noticing that she was often sent down to the river, a wooden bucket in each hand, he would follow, suddenly appearing after she had filled them and offering to carry them. Her initial reluctance to accept his help lessened.

"Have you always lived here, Raisa?" asked Matous as they walked back one evening, the sinking sun casting shafts of soft light amongst the tree trunks.

"Yes, I was born here and will probably die here."

"Do you never wish you could see some of the world?"

"Sometimes. I have wondered about jumping aboard a passing train once or twice, but where would I go and what would I do? My family are here, they are my world. I'd miss them, just like you must miss your home and family.

"Yes." Matous didn't reveal that such concerns were no longer at the forefront of his mind.

Only a few weeks after their arrival, the Legionnaires awoke to ice on the inside of the windows, stuck there like frozen feathers. Outside, a hoar frost held the world in a paralysing grip which it would only begin to release once the sun rose above the tree tops. It was beautiful, but a vicious beauty. In Siberia, the transition between seasons could be precipitate. The days were shortening more quickly daily, and soon today would feel warm and light compared to the extreme cold and long dark nights to come. The Legionnaires swapped their summer caps for fur hats and donned fur coats reaching nearly to the ground which had recently arrived with the supply train. They wrapped scarves around their faces so that only their eyes were uncovered and exposed to the freezing elements.

When snow fell it intensified the quiet that encircled them, interrupted only by the crisp crunching sound which their boots made as they patrolled the railway line. At night, the howls of wolves took on a more haunting quality and the myriad of stars above twinkled in a teasing manner, completely out of reach exactly as was Prague.

Each time the men would see a train coming down the rails, black smoke pouring from it as if a smouldering caldera, they would melt into the forest, manning their guns and ready to fire if need be. However, they needn't have feared. That winter the Czechs remained in charge of the Trans Siberian. It was a remarkable achievement. Men from a small, insignificant land in control of the west-east artery of the world's largest country.

In November, one train brought news that caused the men to erupt with joy. The war in Europe had ended, and the Austro-Hungarian Empire had collapsed like a pack of cards. On 28 October 1918, Czechoslovakia had become an independent nation. Joined by the soldiers from the train, the men held an impromptu celebration, linking arms and dancing by the side of the tracks before climbing aboard to toast their new country with the crew's plentiful supply of vodka, the one thing which Russia didn't seem to have a shortage of.

More than a little inebriated, they staggered back to the village singing raucously, some receiving an abrupt reckoning for over indulging when they fell face down in the snow. Raisa and another young woman who were coming down the track, stood aside to let them pass.

"Dance with us," shouted one of the soldiers. "We've our own country now."

The women shrank back. The man lurched at Raisa, grabbing her arm.

"What's wrong? Think you're too good for me, is that it?"

"Leave her alone." Matous moved towards the man.

"Huh, Rubinstein, a filthy Jew just like these bitches."

Matous launched himself at the man and they fell to the ground, wrestling for supremacy.

"Stop that, immediately!" It was the voice of Smolek, their commander. "You're a disgrace to your country, both of you. Any more of this behaviour and I'll have you both locked up in a barn for the night."

"Are you all right?" asked Stefan once they had reached the house which they shared with six other Legionnaires. The others gave Matous stares which bordered on hostility.

"I'm fine. But I wonder about this new country of Czechoslovakia we apparently have, whether it will be any different, any better than what we had before."

"Of course it will, we're free to be Czechs and be true to our culture."

"Yes, you are and others like you. But for people like me and Rudi, I'm not so sure."

"You're just upset about that buffoon Belinsky. He's had too much to drink."

"That's often when people's true feelings come out. I'm going to see if I can find Raisa and check on her."

Matous walked through the village as dusk descended and the cloudless sky presaged another bitterly cold night. He stopped outside Raisa's family home. Its steeply sloping roof already carried a thick headdress of snow. The glow of candlelight silhouetted the warmth of a loving family through the window. He walked towards their door but halted, what was he thinking? He was an outsider here too. The villagers might let him attend their synagogue but he wasn't one of them and never would be.

One day, maybe one day soon, he would be leaving, leaving without Raisa. Morose at the prospect, he retreated and spent a largely sleepless night.

His spirits rose the following morning when he spotted her through an open barn door, outlined by rays of sunshine which pierced the gaps in the wooden walls. Seated on a low stool, she was milking the family's cow. Matous walked in and gave a cough to attract her attention. Raisa looked up.

"I'm sorry about yesterday."

"It was harmless enough but thank you for what you did."

"There's something I need to ask you. We could receive orders at any time to move out." Raisa stood up and backed away a little as if sensing what he was going to say. "Raisa, I've fallen in love with you. I-"

"I can't," she said determined not to let him finish. "I'm betrothed to Ezekiel. My parents arranged it a few days ago."

Matous looked horrified. "But he's an old man, an old man whose beard is the colour of snow. You can't possibly love him." Raisa looked down at the ground for a moment. "I knew it. Marry me instead, I can make you happy in a way he never can."

"Matous, you have to understand, I don't have a choice." Matous thought he saw tears pool in her eyes. He moved forwards to take her hands but Raisa backed away. "We weren't meant to be, you must accept that. Please go."

Her lips narrowed and her eyes held out no hint of hope.

CHAPTER 11

When spring came after a winter that had seemed never ending, it remained winter in Matous' heart. He and Raisa hadn't spoken since their conversation in the barn. When their paths crossed, which wasn't often these days, Raisa averted her eyes. Matous longed to leave and get far away from the torment of living here, get home where he could forget about Raisa.

On the day of Raisa's wedding he was relieved to be out on patrol, but he wasn't looking forward to returning to the village. There would be singing and dancing lasting well into the night, and Raisa would forever be out of his reach.

Matous decided that when they got back he would go off into the forest for the evening to be alone. He didn't feel like talking, not even to Stefan. His friend had tried to be of comfort, had told him that although it might not seem like it now he would meet someone when they got back to Prague. Matous hadn't contradicted him, withdrawing inside himself and pretending all was well and that he was over her. That way Stefan wouldn't keep asking him how he was, and wouldn't need to tell him again that he would soon feel so much better.

The Legionnaires trudged back along the side of the railway track after yet another uneventful day. Uneventful, thought Matous, that was the problem. Nothing ever happened here in this remote outpost on the way to nowhere. If only they had been stationed in Irkutsk life could have been interesting. It was a city, the Paris of Siberia they called it. Doubtless a poor substitute for the real one, yet the nearest thing there was to civilisation in this godforsaken land where man was overwhelmed by wilderness and there was nothing to stimulate the mind.

At first, Matous was unperturbed by the smoke rising above the trees. The wedding would be in full swing and the food cooking. Yet he soon began to question why there should be more than one plume of smoke and why they were blacker and thicker than any he had ever seen in the village. Others had noticed too, their brows creasing with concern.

"Something's not right," said Matous and he began to run.

"Stop!" shouted Smolek. "We could be running into a trap. We must advance with caution."

To Matous, their progress seemed to be at a snail's pace. Every second taken was increasing the chance of them being too late to save Raisa. As they neared the settlement, Smolek indicated with his arm that they should proceed through the forest to avoid ambush.

Reaching the edge of the tree cover, devastation greeted them. Not a building remained untouched, each one had been set on fire. The long table set up for the wedding breakfast was on its side, the wildflowers with which it had been decorated strewn on the earth and crushed underfoot. Bodies lay scattered, shot as they had tried to run for cover.

Smolek emerged first and signalled for the rest to follow. They moved through the village with lupine stealth, taking cover behind smouldering pyres which only earlier that day had been the villagers' homes. Matous retched when he saw the corpse of Raisa's mother. Raisa's body must surely be close by.

One man was lying face up, a vermilion circle of blood on his tunic. The same man who had asked them to leave the day they had arrived. Barely clinging to life, he snatched irregular gasps of air. Smolek crouched down beside him.

"What happened?"

The man raised his head slightly, wincing as he did so. His speech was laboured.

"The Bolsheviks came... came to punish us for harbouring the enemy, they said. I told you... told you couldn't protect us."

"Did they kill everyone?"

"All save for the young women. They took them with them when they left. It would have been better for them if they had died too." He let his head fall back to the ground, exhausted from the effort.

"Sir, we must go and rescue them. They can't be far away," urged Matous.

"We will do no such thing," said Smolek standing up. "We shall secure our position here and wait for the next train to come."

"But, sir-" protested Matous.

"Enough. Right men, clear these bodies and bury them."

Matous ran his hand through his hair with anguish, he had to do something. He glanced around. His comrades were already absorbed in their task. Gingerly he moved away towards the forest and the footprints left in the mud.

A firm hand fell on his shoulder. "Matous, it's too late. You can't do this, you're disobeying orders."

Matous turned to face Stefan. "I've got to save her. It doesn't take much imagination to know why they only spared the young women."

"You'll never succeed alone."

"Maybe not, but I've got to try."

"Come on then."

"You don't have to do this, Stefan."

"Yes, I do. I'm not abandoning my best friend when he needs me most."

It was late afternoon when they caught up with them. The track they had left with their footprints had moved back towards the railway line. Through the pine trees, the two friends could see the backs of the six young women seated on the ground, hands tied behind them. One was dressed in white, a bride already a widow on her wedding day. Beyond them their captors, maybe ten in total, lay on the ground not far back from the railway line, waiting like predators and ready to leap onto their prey when it appeared. It was clear that they had placed explosives on the track which they would detonate when a train came.

"We need to go down the track, one of us in each direction to warn the first train we see," whispered Stefan.

"We must free Raisa and the others first," insisted Matous.

"We can't. If we're spotted and killed who is going to warn the next train?"

"I'm not leaving her here."

"Matous, if the worst has happened, it's happened already. We can rescue them when we have stopped a train."

"No." Matous was adamant.

"You're on your own then. A train could be coming down the track right now, and if it's not halted many of our men are going to die."

Stefan didn't wait for Matous' response and hurried off eastwards through the trees. Matous crouched down with indecision. If he was caught while trying to free the women, he would be guilty of causing the death of those on the next train coming from the west.

CHAPTER 12

Matous put his finger to his lips to indicate silence was required. He could tell immediately from her eyes which saw him but didn't react that he was already too late. Her torn dress of satin and lace confirmed it. His heart thumping against his ribcage, his fingers fumbling, he untied Raisa's hands and then her feet before freeing the others.

"Follow the track back to the village, the soldiers are there," he said in a quiet voice. "Here take my coat."

He placed it around her shoulders. Raisa said nothing, nor did the others. Matous watched them go, anxiously also looking in the other direction every few seconds, worried one of the Bolsheviks might turn. He wouldn't survive if they did but he might be able to create enough of a delay for Raisa to escape. The young women went without speed or any show of relief that they had been freed. The moment that they were out of sight Matous too departed, moving out onto the side of the railway line once he couldn't be seen by the Soviets.

He had gone less than a kilometre when he heard that familiar noise. As it rounded the bend ahead of him, Matous leapt into the middle of the track, frantically waving his arms above his head like a man possessed. In a cloud of steam and with a grating of brakes, the train slowed. Soldiers jumped off, their rifles pointed at him.

"Don't shoot!"

"What the hell are you doing here?" It was Smolek.

"The Bolsheviks have set an ambush. They are waiting for you up ahead. I can lead you through the forest so we can attack them from the rear."

Quietly as a Siberian tiger, the men approached their unsuspecting enemy who, if they had noticed that the women had escaped, had failed to guard their rear. The assault was short and furious. Curses at being taken by surprise and a hail of bullets filled the air. The Russians didn't have time to return fire.

"Back to the train everyone," ordered Smolek when it was over.

"Sir, I sent the women they kidnapped back to the village. We can't leave them there," pleaded Matous.

"It's lucky for you, Rubinstein, that it's turned out the way it has or you would be facing a firing squad. You can go fetch them. But be quick, we can't hang around. We're retreating to Irkutsk. The Reds are everywhere, and they're thrashing the White Army."

Matous raced all the way. The expression of Raisa and the other women when he relayed the news remained a vacant one. The light in their eyes had been extinguished, their lives changing forever in the space of a few terrible hours, the memories of which would haunt them probably for the rest of their lives.

Smolek was pacing up and down impatiently when Matous returned with the women. The train didn't go far before it stopped again, this time for Stefan. The two friends embraced, each delighted the other had survived.

"Well done, Matous, you're a hero," said Stefan after hearing what had happened. But Matous felt no joy. He needed to talk with her.

Raisa and the others were huddled in the far corner of a carriage, heads down. They didn't look up as he approached. Matous halted, what was he supposed to say, what could he say? He turned and went back the way he had come.

When the train reached Irkutsk, one of the women asked a station employee the way to the Jewish quarter and they departed not once looking back, their heads still hung in trauma and shame. The men were marched through the streets to the barracks.

For the first time, it registered with the soldiers that they were deep in the heart of Asia. The domes of churches and their brightly coloured facades might be Russian Orthodox but there was variety in the faces of the inhabitants, many were of Mongolian and Chinese heritage. However, the men were not particularly interested in their new surroundings. The enthusiasm and sense of pride which they had once felt at doing their bit had gone. This wasn't their war and they had their own country now. Rumours abounded, bouncing off the walls of the dormitory and bringing gloom. The Reds had the city surrounded. Legionnaires farther west were cut off. The line to Vladivostok was blocked by the Soviets. The last of the Allied ships had already left the port.

"Maybe we should try to break out and go south to Mongolia, apparently it's less than two hundred kilometres to the border, and from there make our way to China and the coast," suggested Stefan one afternoon while a group of them fished by the banks of the Angara river, which flows through the city, to supplement their unsatisfactory rations. A large statue of the last Tsar's father, Alexander III, built to thank him for ordering the building of the Trans Siberian and bringing prosperity to this city, stood nearby casting a shadow upon them for overstaying their welcome.

"And end up being killed by bandits," responded another.

"Well, do you have a better idea? We're still four thousand kilometres from Vladivostok. The Bolsheviks will overrun us if we remain here, and

I doubt they take prisoners. I'm sure they'd like revenge. Without us holding the railway, the Whites would have been beaten long ago. And I've heard tell we have here in Irkutsk eight wagons of the Tsar's gold which other Legionnaires captured early in the conflict."

"That sounds like good news to me, it gives us something to bargain with."

And it would. Their leaders were able to negotiate an armistice, handing over the White Army leader, Admiral Kolchak, and the Tsar's gold in return for unmolested passage across the remainder of Siberia to Vladivostok. It is alleged the Czechs kept one wagon of gold for themselves taking it back to Prague to fund the national bank, but no evidence to support that claim has ever been uncovered.

Matous wasn't by the river. He was hurrying across town to the Jewish ghetto, purpose in his stride. Time was short, he didn't anticipate the army would be staying much longer. Timber buildings lined the streets, suspended between charm and decline. Their painted shutters and intricate carved designs above the windows like wooden lace were attractive but he hadn't noticed them.

Asking around, Matous found where she was living. The blue and white shutters were cheerful, but the interior was dark and dismal. Her cousin, who opened the door, made her excuses and disappeared into the other room.

"Hello, Raisa."

She got up from a chair. "Matous. I wasn't expecting to see you."

"We're leaving in a few days and going home."

"You must be pleased."

"I would be if you were coming. Marry me, Raisa, come back to Prague with me as my wife."

"I can't."

"Your parents are with God now. What do you have to stay for? The Bolsheviks are winning, they'll be here soon. You won't be safe with them around."

"I can't marry you or any man, I'd only bring shame." She placed a hand on her stomach. "There's a Russian's child growing inside of me."

CHAPTER 13

Matous swayed slightly and placed his hand across his mouth and chin as he absorbed Raisa's announcement.

"I'm sorry, Matous." She had expected him to leave yet he remained. There was no disdain in his eyes, only sympathy and understanding.

"You have no need to apologise. It wasn't your fault, and it makes no difference to how I feel about you. We can pretend the child's mine, no one need ever know."

"You deserve better, and one day you might come to resent the child as well as me."

"No, I won't. I promise." Still confused and hesitant, Raisa exhaled. "Say yes, Raisa. Say yes."

They married in the synagogue, a large wooden building painted in soft yellow and turquoise, with the external appearance of a minor palace. Only Stefan and Raisa's cousin attended the wedding. Raisa's dress was loose fitting to hide her growing stomach and she didn't smile during the ceremony. Afterwards, the four of them went to eat in one of the city's Chinese restaurants. It wasn't the kind of wedding either bride or bridegroom had imagined would be theirs, but that didn't bother Matous. He had succeeded, the chase was over and Raisa was his.

The wedding made Stefan's desire to return to Prague and Dagmar even stronger. Matous was married and no doubt Rudi too by now. Stefan couldn't wait to marry his first and only love.

The journey to Vladivostok was long and nerve-wracking. Each time the train came to a halt, those it carried worried why. The passengers inside sat in expectant silence, faces drawn, waiting for gunfire to erupt at any moment. Nagging doubts that the Bolsheviks would never let them go resurfaced. Finally, they reached the Pacific. A journey across Russia that should have taken less than two weeks had ultimately lasted nearly two years.

When the train rounded the last hill, it was for the vast majority of them the first time they had seen the ocean. Like a lake without end, somewhere out there was their route home. Ships' funnels stood tall above the harbour as if factory chimneys. Marched from the station, the men passed the Tsar's triumphal arch built to commemorate his visit in 1891. Back then, as heir to the throne, he had been obliged to travel from Saint Petersburg to southern Europe and then by boat via the Suez Canal to get here to lay the foundation stone for the project to build the world's longest railway. Local folklore said that anyone who passed under the arch would be happy. The soldiers were routed around it.

Gratefully, the men boarded a huge American troop carrier. As they entered its protection, Stefan and Matous both breathed a sigh of relief. They had escaped mother Russia's domineering embrace and were en route home. Raisa and other wives, of which there were several, boarded separately. They were to pass the voyage in another part of the boat.

Stefan soon decided a river, like the Vltava, was the only water he ever wanted to see again. With the almost constant rolling and pitching and the inescapable stench of vomit, crossing oceans was an experience he didn't want to repeat.

In San Diego, they were transferred to another ship going to Europe. As they passed through the Panama Canal, Matous received word that Raisa had given birth to a boy. Permitted to visit them, Raisa watched intently as Matous took the baby from her arms. Whether his awkwardness reflected his inexperience with infants or an attempt to conceal revulsion at the physical embodiment of her rape, she couldn't tell.

Raisa already loved the child. He made her experience easier to bear, something so perfect and beautiful that had come from something so vile. For a long time, she hadn't wanted to continue living. The murder of her family and the violent assault on her had plunged Raisa into the deepest pit of despair. Even at her wedding she had felt sadness. She would have welcomed death had it come, but no longer. The pain of the loss of her family would always be there but now she refused to give her attackers the final victory. Her son would be her ladder to climb up and out of those dark places which she had inhabited these last nine months.

They agreed to name him Yosef after Raisa's father. That evening the men toasted Matous, most horizontally from their hammocks hung with barely a gap between them. Matous thanked them and smiled a smile which only Stefan knew wasn't genuine.

Reaching Europe some weeks later, all were on deck to watch their arrival in Trieste. Yet it was a Europe so different from the one they had left. Once the significant port of the Austro-Hungarian Empire, and a naval base for a navy which they no longer had, Trieste was now part of Italy. The Empire had been dismantled by the victors.

A train to Vienna and only the final leg remained, a short stop at an army base on the outskirts of Prague and then home. As the train approached Prague conversation subsided. Excited anticipation filled the carriage. The place Stefan had dreamed of so many times these past six years, only to wake to an empty reality and an aching inside, was only minutes away.

As they pulled into the station, now renamed Wilson Station after the US President who had led international support for the creation of Czechoslovakia, Stefan scanned the platform hoping to see Dagmar and his parents. He had written from the boat but couldn't give a date or time that he would arrive, and he was probably back before the letter in any event. They weren't there but it didn't matter, he would be reunited with them all before the end of the day.

Stefan couldn't stop smiling as he walked through his city of dreams, looking up frequently to drink in the stunning architecture that characterised Prague. Irkutsk contained pockets of charm, San Diego had sunshine and palm trees, and Vienna was grand, yet Prague was without doubt the queen of them all. He had been right around the world but no other city could hold a candle to his own.

At first, nothing appeared to have changed during his absence, save for the most important thing. The double-headed eagle of the Austro-Hungarian Empire had flown. From many buildings fluttered the red, white and blue flag of Czechoslovakia. Like the former Empire, the new country too would have its fault lines. The Slovaks would be the junior partner, much smaller in terms of population and poorer too without the developed industry of the Czech half. And Germans, who made up over a fifth of the population, were unhappy not to be part of Austria or Germany. However, none of that yet troubled the country's dominant city and capital, still euphoric at freedom from foreign domination.

When he reached the Old Town Square, Stefan noticed that the forty-five meter high Marian column topped by the Virgin Mary in the centre of the square had gone. Nearby a large new bronze statue had been erected to Czech hero, Jan Hus, burned at the stake in the fifteenth century by Catholic rulers for his Reformation beliefs. Hus stood tall and proud above smaller figures of Hussite warriors and Protestants who had been exiled.

As Stefan walked across Charles bridge, his heart overflowed with happiness at the sight of the castle complex on the hill above Mala Strana, and at the far end of the bridge the archway between the two towers that would lead him home to his family. Despite his focus on getting there, he did notice one thing close at ground level which had altered. Apart from old ladies clinging to tradition, the hem line had risen to mid-calf. Ankles and lower legs were on full display. Stefan liked the change. It represented another break with the past, a modernity that seemed right after the overthrow of the stuffy old order and the war to end all wars.

Walking across the main square in Mala Strana, he was surprised that the statue of Marshal Radecky - immortalised by Strauss' Radetzky March - had also disappeared.

Stefan bounded up the stairs to his parents' apartment and knocked. He couldn't wait to see their smiles and embrace them both. Surprised not to get an answer, he knocked again but still the door didn't open. He turned the handle.

"Hello?"

There was no response. Perhaps his mother was out shopping. Stefan breathed in the familiar smell of home but somehow it wasn't quite the same. Something was missing but he wasn't sure what. Maybe it was the rich aroma of coffee or the smell of freshly baked bread which was lacking.

Stefan went down to the workshop and pushed open the door. His father was sitting on his stool at the bench, hunched closer than ever to his work.

"Tatka."

The old man turned slowly.

"My son." He choked with emotion as he uttered the words. Rising, he entered Stefan's outstretched arms. "At last, at last." He pulled back to look a his boy. "It's been so long, we thought you were dead. It was awful not knowing. It was long after independence that we got word you were thought to be still alive."

"Well, I'm here now, back for good. Where's Mamka, she's not upstairs."

His father let go of Stefan's arms, his face shorn of the happiness seeing his son had brought. "She is with God."

CHAPTER 14

Dead?" Tears stung Stefan's eyes and he gulped air as he fought to suppress guttural sobs that came from deep within him.

"Come sit down." Like a child, Stefan let his father lead him to the stool next to the workbench.

"When?" Stefan asked after he had regained his composure.

"A month ago, Spanish flu. It has killed so many in Prague."

Stefan hung his head. If only he could have made it home earlier to see her one last time. It had never entered his mind that he would be too late.

"Let's go upstairs. I'll get you something to eat."

"No, thank you. I'm not hungry. Where is she buried? I want to go there."

It seemed wrong to Stefan that the sky was blue and fluffy white clouds were floating happily past as he stood at his mother's grave. The world should be crying with him. It should be grey with heavy rain. He laid the flowers he had brought and said a silent prayer. So many times in Russia he had imagined his homecoming. It had never been like this.

Stefan postponed his plans to visit Dagmar. Today was no longer what he had thought it would be. Even the church bells tolling that evening seemed different. In Siberia, he had heard them in his mind, a sound which was joyful and life affirming. Now their toll to him was profoundly solemn, a requiem for his mother, and for all the death which he had encountered these past few years.

That evening, they dined on mushroom soup and bread. The soup lacked flavour and the bread had an odd taste. It seemed his father must have forgotten to add salt. Stefan realised that not only did their home feel empty without his mother but that her absence would announce itself in so many different ways.

I'm glad to have you back," said his father as he slurped his last spoonful. "I don't seem able to get things done so quickly as I used to and I'm behind with the rent."

"Money is one worry we won't have," Stefan assured his father. "The army owes me back pay and I have some saved. There was little to spend it on in Siberia."

"What was it like there?"

"I'll tell you one day but I don't feel like talking about it tonight. Tell me, what's happened to the Virgin in Old Town Square and Marshal Radecky here in Mala Strana," said Stefan changing the subject.

"It's a sign of the times. A couple of years ago a group of young Czechs pulled the Virgin's column down. They said it represented Hapsburg oppression and the supremacy of the Catholic Church. You'd have thought they'd have been happy that the city erected a huge memorial in the very same square to Jan Hus the year after you left, but clearly it wasn't enough for them."
"I wondered who the new statue was for, it's big."
"And as for Radecky, despite being a Czech and such a famous soldier, it was thought he too represented the Empire, having fought for them like everyone once did. They covered him in a black cloth for a while before removing him. But enough about monuments, what about Dagmar, have you been to see her?"
"No, I came straight here. I'll go soon."

On Kampa Island, the atmosphere in the dining room at the Rubinstein's was not as Matous had expected it would be. The conversation was stilted and sparse, the clink of cutlery on crockery loud.
When he had arrived home, his parents had tried to disguise their shock with awkward smiles and a peck on the cheek given to Raisa at arms' length, but his mother hadn't asked to hold Yosef. While Raisa and baby slept, Matous' mother cornered him in the drawing room.
"Father and I are so pleased you're home safe, though I must say you've given us quite a sur-

prise. Getting married, and a baby too. Did she trick you into marriage?"

"No, I love her."

"Mmm." His mother didn't sound convinced. "Have you thought how hard life will be here for her? She can only speak a few words of Czech."

"She'll learn, I'm teaching her."

"Maybe but a city life isn't what's she is used to. She's a country girl, from Siberia of all places. You can't get more remote than that."

"Exactly what are you trying to say."

"Just that we wanted more for you."

"How? I have a beautiful wife and child. Why can't you be happy for me?" Matous stormed from the room, slamming the door as he went.

Two days later, Stefan made his way up to the castle. Tomas Masaryk, who had led his country to independence, resided there now as President. Not everyone welcomed that, particularly those of German heritage. He had denounced Germans in the country as colonists and settlers, something which affirmed their belief they didn't belong in this new country.

Stefan's emotions were mixed as he reached Novy Svet. His happiness should have been about to reach its zenith, but his mother wouldn't get to see him marry or meet her grandchildren. The trepidation he might once have felt at knocking on Dagmar's front door and revealing to her mother that her daughter and he were in love no longer existed. His mother's death had put things into perspective. Dagmar's mother was not going to stand in their way, of that he was determined.

After six years, Stefan hadn't expected Dagmar's mother to recognise him but she did and it still failed to produce a smile on her part.

"I've come to see Dagmar."

"Have you. Wait there a moment."

Stefan's pulse raced with excitement, only seconds now until he saw his love.

The woman didn't return with Dagmar. "You can have this back." She thrust Stefan's opened letter into his hand. "She won't want this, she's a married woman."

Stefan was stunned. "Married?"

"You heard me." The woman slammed the door shut.

CHAPTER 15

Unable to believe her words, Stefan rubbed his forehead hard with the fingers of his right hand and then remained immobile as if turned to stone. When he began to make his way home, the heaviness in his heart grew until it felt like a boulder weighing him down.

Self pity promised him a shoulder to cry on so he stopped at a bar and got drunk. Navigating the cobbles afterwards proved a challenge. He had fallen over twice by the time he reached his father's front door. Stefan didn't open it. Instead, he slid down the wall adjacent to it and fell asleep on the floor.

"What happened to you?" asked his father, discovering the crumpled heap of Stefan the following morning.

Stefan opened his eyes a little, squinting as he did so. "I drunk too much."

"And Dagmar?"

"She married someone else while I was away."

"That's too bad, but don't worry there's plenty more fish in the sea. Marek Lanik, across the street, has a daughter, Marta. She's a fine young woman. You should say hello to her." Stefan groaned and curled up in a ball. Tact was another thing which his mother had possessed and his father didn't. "I'm going down to the workshop, but I suggest you go sleep it off."

Stefan slept until noon. He decided to visit Matous.

"Do you mind if we go for a walk?" asked Matous when he opened the front door. "Raisa and the baby are sleeping, and I need to get away from my parents."

"Oh dear, weren't they pleased to see you?"

"Me, yes. Not Raisa and Yosef. They think I've married below my station. And I think mother suspects Yosef's not mine. I'm going to see an apartment in the Old Town tomorrow, we have to get out of my parents' house. Anyway, enough about my troubles. What about you?"

Stefan stopped walking. "My mother's dead."

"Oh no, I'm so sorry."

"And Dagmar..." Stefan's voice faltered. "She got married."

Matous placed his arm around his friend's shoulder.

They strolled slowly beside the river, neither saying much for some while. Matous resisted the temptation to tell Stefan that he would soon feel better as Stefan had once told him. Now was a time to let grief in so that one day it would get bored and leave.

"I went to see Rudi," said Matous. "But he's moved

out, he's living across the river in the New Town. He has a wife now, his mother said."

"Maybe if I'd been like him and not joined the Legion, I too would have been married." There was a distinct note of envy in Stefan's voice. "They say the prisoners of war have been back for nearly two years. They were able to get on with their lives while we were stuck in Russia helping one evil dictator fight another."

"I can understand how you must feel."

"We should go see Rudi some time. Now things are back to normal, it can be like old times again."

"Yes, one day soon. I should probably be getting back, Raisa doesn't like being left alone with my parents. Any time you want company you know where to find me."

"Thanks, Matous. I think I'll stay here a for a bit." Stefan watched the Vltava flow by, untroubled by his problems, untroubled by anyone's problems. Stefan thought of the summer's day when he had first met his friends at the river and the winter's day out on the ice, that day Dagmar had first captivated him, such happy, uncomplicated days. When would they return or had they gone, swept away by the current, carefree youth replaced by the invisible punches and kicks of adult life?

Stefan's father rarely spoke when they were working so Stefan was able to turn inwards. He created a refuge for himself amongst the wooden world of puppets, working long hours making those whose lives he could control. Hiding in the workshop, he didn't have to go outside and see couples strolling arm in arm, their smiles bright and their laughs heartfelt.

One day his father looked up from his work and stared at Stefan until he could sense it and no longer ignore him.

"I know you've been through a lot, but it's time to stop moping and feeling sorry for yourself. You need to count your blessings. You made it home. Many didn't, and many who did have horrible injuries. I'm going to invite Marek and Marta over for dinner. His wife was also taken by the flu."

Stefan wasn't in the mood for socialising and would rather have stayed in his room but his father insisted. After all, what would his mother have thought of such behaviour, he said.

Marek and Marta arrived on the dot of six. She was still wearing black and was not what Stefan considered beautiful. He thought her rather plain and her nose too big, yet her face was round and cheerful and her eyes were warm and kind.

"We're delighted to meet you," said Marek. "Your father must be so proud of you, a hero. You boys in the Legion are a legend, single-handedly taking over half of Russia. Without your bravery, we may never have got the support of the Allies to create our own country."

Stefan reddened, he had never considered himself to be a hero.

The evening was surprisingly convivial even if

his father's cooking reflected his lack of experience in the kitchen, and Stefan's input to the meal hadn't improved it either. Marta taught at the local school and asked whether Stefan and his father might consider coming one day to do a puppet show. To Stefan's surprise, his father said yes.

Lifted out of his doldrums a little by the previous evening, Stefan went over to see Matous and Raisa in their new home located in one of the narrow backstreets of the Old Town.

"Come in," Matous welcomed him. "What do you think?"

"It's as small as where I live."

"Indeed it is but it's our own space."

"And how are you, Raisa? I see little Yosef's grown." He already looked about as much as his mother could hold. A stocky baby with a low forehead, fair hair and blue eyes, he bore no resemblance to Matous.

"I'm fine, thanks. I'll let you two talk, I need to change him." Raisa disappeared into the bedroom.

"So how are you, Stefan? Your father told me you didn't want to see anyone the day I called by with our new address."

"Better, thanks. It's time to put the past behind me and move on. I was thinking we should go see Rudi and his new wife."

"I went to see them the other week. There's something you need to know."

"What?" Matous' expression was too serious for Stefan's liking.

"Rudi married Dagmar."

CHAPTER 16

The information was like a hot needle through his brain. Stefan clutched the sides of his head in disbelief.

"Why? How could they do that to me?"

"They thought you were dead."

Stefan wasn't persuaded. "They didn't know that. They would have heard of the Legion, everyone in Prague did. They must surely have considered the possibility that I might be in it, unable to get home. She promised to wait. He was a friend, we saved his life."

"I realise it must be a shock."

"Yes, it's a monumental one, betrayed by two people I trusted." Matous put a hand on Stefan's arm but he threw it off. "Where do they live?"

The feral anger in Stefan's eyes concerned Matous. "You're upset. Now is not the time-"

"So even you, my best friend, won't help me, huh?" Stefan threw him a look of contempt and left.

Marta and Stefan married a few months later in the Church of Our Lady of Victory. St Nicholas was much too large for their small wedding party. Kneeling before its famous inhabitant, the Bambino di Praga, an effigy of Jesus as a three year old kept in a glass case, they said their wedding vows. Shipped from Spain hundreds of years earlier, the effigy is said to perform miracles and answer prayers, not that Stefan asked him for anything although he suspected Marta did as he observed her praying, eyes tightly shut and her lips moving in silent utterance.

Children from Marta's school held her bridal train and sang for the couple. Matous acted as Stefan's best man and played an excerpt from Dvorak's violin concerto. Marta thought it a perfect day.

Stefan wasn't sure if the real reason that he was marrying Marta was a pointless act of spite to let Dagmar know that she meant nothing to him. Whatever he married for, he wasn't marrying for love. He was fond of Marta but she didn't make his pulse race and his stomach flutter as Dagmar once had.

After the ceremony, the wedding party moved to a nearby restaurant. The owner greeted them by breaking a plate which is supposed to bring happiness, and the bride and groom followed the tradition of eating soup together with one spoon.

Stefan's father moved into his son's room and gave the newlyweds his own larger bedroom.

Meanwhile Matous was accepted into the Czech Philharmonic Orchestra and often away on tour.

The orchestra had lost its original home at the Rudolfinum. The building with its facade of Ionic columns and a curving balustrade with statues of musicians had been converted into the Czechoslovak Parliament but there was no resentment. It was the seat of their democracy, their heady new world of freedom and a source of great pride.

The city grew ever outwards, making suburbs of villages as many from other parts of the country migrated there seeking a better life. Both Matous and Stefan and their wives contributed to the population increase. Marta gave birth to a son, Pavel, and a daughter, Klara. Their birth brought Stefan the sense of unbridled joy which marriage had failed to. The new Republic enshrined equal rights for women in its constitution but in practice not much changed, and Marta was obliged to give up her teaching job.

Raisa produced another boy, Jakub. Matous tried not to prefer him to Yosef but he did. Whenever Matous looked at that boy, seeing not one trace of himself reminded him of how Yosef had been conceived.

Busy earning a living and raising families, the two friends saw each other infrequently. They attended reunions of the Legion and marched into Wenceslas Square, proudly wearing their medals for the annual Independence Day celebrations. In a Kafkaesque manner, although many more Czechs had fought and died for the Emperor than the Legion, that fact was conveniently ignored. Kafka, recently deceased, had himself been a Prague resident and a German speaking Jew, which neatly encapsulated the nuances of the city.

Time passed quickly. Working long hours and looking after young children seemed to accelerate its progress.

It was one warm afternoon that Stefan and Marta sat enjoying a coffee at an outdoor cafe in the Old Town opposite the Old Town Hall. The children were waiting patiently in front of it for the hour to change so they could watch the two doors above the medieval astronomical clock on the tower open and see figures of the twelve apostles parade before finally an automated cockerel would pop out and flap its wings. The clock was about to strike when Stefan saw her pass by, walking briskly and in a focused manner. His heart missed a beat, and a little devil on his shoulder told him to seize the moment or it might never come again. He jumped up from his chair.

"I've just remembered that I promised to deliver some puppets to the theatre today. Do you mind taking the children home without me?"

"Not at all," smiled Marta. "They're your best customer. We'll see you later."

Stefan ran down a side street to catch her and called her name. He could see that she recognised him the moment she turned.

"How are you?"

"Well enough, thank you."

"Can you meet me for a coffee?" he blurted out.

Dagmar's look was one of disapproval. "Stefan, you're a married man."

"I am but I think I deserve an explanation. Just ten minutes, that's all I ask. Please."

His voice was loud and attracting the attention of others. Embarrassed, Dagmar relented.

"All right. Tomorrow, at eleven at Cafe Slavia."

Dagmar was already there when he arrived, seated by one of the tall picture windows which afforded a fine view across the river and up towards the castle. One of Prague's iconic sights, the roof and spires of St Vitus Cathedral standing proudly above the unbroken wall of palaces which surrounded it.

"I really do have only ten minutes," she said as he gave her an uncertain smile and sat down.

"I won't beat around the bush then. Why didn't you wait for me, Dagmar, like you said you would?"

"I didn't think you'd be gone so long. I was young, confused. I... I felt bad about you going off to war with me not having accepted your proposal. I thought you needed hope."

"Hope? So I meant nothing to you, and you married Rudi instead."

"I didn't plan it like that. We bumped into each other purely by chance shortly after he returned and - anyway, I'm sure Matous must have told you that we've separated."

"No, he hasn't."

"We just weren't suited."

Stefan felt emboldened. "Dagmar, I'm still in love with you." He put his hand out towards hers, but she moved her hand off the table.

"Stefan, you can't be."

"I am. I like my wife but I don't love her."

"I'm not looking for love. I want to make a difference and do something meaningful with my life. I'm not the girl you knew. I'm going to be running for election to Parliament. It's one of the reasons Rudi and I broke up. He didn't approve of women having a career, especially his own wife."

"I'm not like that."

"Aren't you?" Dagmar sounded unconvinced. "I'm not going to break up a marriage. To be brutally honest, Stefan, I don't love you and I don't think I ever really did. I must be going. You should cherish what you have. Whoever you imagine me to be, I am not that person."

CHAPTER 17

Stefan stayed long after Dagmar had left, staring into his empty coffee cup.

Deflated, he arranged to meet Matous one evening for a beer. Matous greeted him inside the small, narrow bar with a dark wood interior which had heard the conversations and confessions of drinkers for hundreds of years. "How are you, my friend? Long time no see."

Stefan swallowed a mouthful of beer and licked his lips to remove the froth from them. "I saw Dagmar the other day."

"Surely you're not still thinking of her."

Stefan ignored his comment. "Why didn't you tell me she and Rudi had separated?"

"I saw no point. You have a lovely wife and family."

"So do you, Matous, but I'm not sure you're happy," Stefan challenged him.

"I'm away travelling with the orchestra a lot. Last week it was London, the month before Paris. Raisa and I spend a lot of time apart, and yes I'll admit to you that my marriage isn't what I thought it would be. Things felt different in Siberia. I suppose mother was right - not that I've married beneath myself - but that we weren't really suited. I'm an intellectual, I suppose, and she isn't. I love music, literature and art but Raisa has different interests. In fact, she doesn't really have any apart from the children."

"And you've met someone else."

"How did you guess?" Matous hadn't mentioned his relationship to anyone, not even his best friend.

"It's not hard, we've known each other a long time. Someone in the orchestra no doubt."

"Yes. Radmila's her name."

"Yet you judge me."

"You're right, what you do is your business."

"Well, you needn't worry about my marriage. Dagmar's career minded, intent on becoming a politician of all things. She couldn't have been franker. Told me she didn't have feelings for me, wasn't sure if she ever really did."

"Life isn't what we thought it would be before the war, is it? Still, life is good in so many ways," said Matous.

"I'll drink to that. What's Rudi up to? Was he devastated?"

"No, not really. I think they both accepted that they'd made a mistake. He's very into the German cause. He still hankers after the Empire or union with Germany. I told him if he felt that way then maybe he should move there. He didn't like that. Prague's his home, he said, and the

Czechs should stop treating Germans like they're not wanted. Being a Jew, I can relate to how that feels."

"What will you and Raisa do?" asked Stefan.

"Soldier on, for the sake of the children and the one to come."

"To come?"

"Yes, Raisa is expecting again."

Stefan wasn't sure if congratulations were right in the circumstances so he didn't offer them.

"Does she know about Radmila?"

"I haven't told her, but you know how intuitive women can be. Sometimes I feel bad for having taken Raisa away from Russia. She seems to miss it so. I can't think why but I suppose it's in her blood like Prague is in ours. I've gone a bit Russian myself, I've joined the Communist Party."

"The Communist Party," repeated Stefan incredulously. "Why?"

"The evil of fascism is growing all over Europe. Franco in Spain, Mussolini in Italy, and now there's talk of Hitler gaining power in Germany. I think only Communism is capable of standing up to the threat."

"What about democracy?"

"I believe she'll be a casualty, unable to withstand the coming clash of ideologies."

"I hope you're wrong about that."

"And anyway what is democracy doing for us right now, so many without jobs? In Russia everyone has a job, a home, and free healthcare.

Isn't that a better way to live? This depression is what capitalism gives us. The poor suffer while the rich get richer. It's not right."

"Time for another drink," said Stefan. Politics was something that didn't particularly interest him.

When he got home that evening, he hugged his wife.

"What are you after?" joked Marta at his uncharacteristic display of affection.

"Nothing. Life is good."

"Yes, we are lucky. Two beautiful and healthy children and we have each other. We should be thankful and never forget our blessings. The children aren't asleep yet, they're hoping you'll read them a story."

"I didn't think I'd find you two still awake," said Stefan on entering their bedroom. "If you want to go to the burning of the winter witches tomorrow night, you need to get a good night's sleep."

Their eyes had closed before he had finished the first page. Stefan kissed their cherub cheeks and smiled. It was probably for the best that Dagmar didn't love him.

The next day, being the last one of April, the family assembled early evening outside St Nicholas and joined the procession carrying an effigy of a witch to the park on Kampa Island. When dusk fell a bonfire was set alight with the witch upon it. Known as Čarodejnice, it signifies that winter is over. Winter was thought to give witches strength, whereas warmth and fire would cause them to go away until the next winter. All over the city that night, bonfires were reflected in the eyes of children entranced by the tradition.

It may have been easy to keep witches at bay, but as the years passed events elsewhere were beginning to cast a dark shadow across the nation that bonfires couldn't banish. Hitler had seized power in Germany and was encouraging the German majority in Czechoslovakia's Sudetenland to agitate to become part of the Third Reich. Czechoslovakia found itself the only remaining democracy in Central and Eastern Europe, small and vulnerable.

Matous and Raisa welcomed a baby girl who they named Sara.

Stefan did see Dagmar again. He stopped outside the newsagents to stare at her. This time, however, she was only a picture in the newspaper. She had succeeded in her goal, winning election to Parliament.

Stefan saw Radmila too, arm in arm with Matous. She was quite stunning, her auburn hair up in an elegant chignon, and her face as delicate as fine porcelain. The two of them were emerging late one evening from the National Theatre, carrying their violin cases. Stefan was across the street, en route home from doing a puppet show, wearily pushing on the long wooden arms of his portable stage on wheels. These days he did shows regularly to supplement the family's income now that his father could no longer see well enough to help in the workshop. Stefan and Matous' eyes met but Matous didn't acknowledge his friend. Stefan was displeased but when he thought about it as he continued his journey, he decided it was better that way. The two families were close friends. How much more awkward it would have been next time they all got together if he had been introduced to Matous' mistress.

"You look exhausted," said Marta when Stefan finally arrived home. "Sit yourself down while I get your dinner from the stove."

"I can't go on like this. I need Paja's help, he's fifteen now."

"Is that really the extent of your ambition for him?" Marta's eyes were hostile as she put his plate on the table.

"What's wrong with being a puppeteer? Am I not good enough for you?"

"There's nothing wrong with it, but Paja's a bright lad. The world should be his oyster. I'm not going to have his education prematurely ended. He could get a scholarship and go to university." Marta had placed her hands defiantly on her hips.

"So meanwhile I must continue to work myself into the ground to put food on the table."

"No, you won't have to. I've started offering myself as a private after school tutor, and already two families want to hire me."

"Hmm." Stefan's reply was a grudging agreement. What his wife said made sense. His son wouldn't have his youth stolen by war as he had, and should have all the opportunities which he hadn't.

CHAPTER 18

In September 1937, Tomas Masaryk, the father of the nation died. Stefan and Marta joined a throng of thousands to pay their respects as the former President laid in state inside the gothic splendour of St Vitus Cathedral. It seemed only fitting that the Czech's greatest hero since Wenceslas should be lying under the same roof as him.

On the day of the funeral, the entire city came to a halt. Black flags fluttered from virtually every building and black banners marked "TGM" hung from the cathedral. Pictures of Masaryk with that distinctive fluffy, white moustache dotted the town and covered the front pages of newspapers. Stefan and Matous donned their Legionnaires' uniform once more and marched with thousands of soldiers and former soldiers behind a solitary gun carriage pulled by horses and on which rested the man's coffin covered by the Czechoslovak flag. Huge crowds several rows deep lined the entire route. As the procession from the castle crossed the river on Manusev bridge which would take them in front of the

Parliament, the Czechoslovak air force flew overhead in tribute.

Later that same month, Stefan's father also died. An era had ended, and Stefan whilst hoping the future would be good, wondered if the halcyon days of peace and freedom of the First Republic could also be drawing to a close.

Only one year later, the chill winds of change blew through Prague. For months Hitler had been threatening war if Sudetenland, the country's borderland regions with Germany and Austria, which itself was now also subsumed within the Reich, weren't handed over. The majority German population had never wanted to be part of Czechoslovakia when it had been created, but with its hilly terrain Sudentenland had given the country the natural defences it otherwise lacked. Despite having entered into a treaty to come to the aid of Czechoslovakia if it were attacked, France didn't want a war and neither did Britain so they pressurised Masaryk's successor, President Benes, to agree to Hitler's demands.

Marta wondered what could possibly have happened when Stefan burst into the apartment, breathless from having run from Malostranske Namesti, the main square in Mala Strana.

"What's going on?" There was a note of anxiety in her voice as she observed Stefan bend forward and plant his hands on his knees as he gasped for air. He was forty-two and no longer a young man.

"A decree of mobilisation has been issued. The government's preparing for war should Germany invade."

"Oh my." Marta brushed her hands against her apron with stress.

"I need to get my old uniform and rifle and report for duty."

"Surely not at your age."

"I'm not that old," he chided her.

Klara got up from the dining table and flung her arms around her father. "Don't go, Tatka."

"I have to, my love. I must defend our homeland. The Nazis are evil, wicked people. But don't you worry, Hitler's a bully and if you stand up to bullies they back down."

"I want to come too," demanded Pavel.

"You can't, you're only seventeen," said Marta without a moment's hesitation.

"Your mother's right, you're too young," agreed Stefan ruffling his son's hair. "I need you to stay here and look after your mother and sister as the man of the house until I get back."

"But-" protested Pavel.

"If you want to be a man, you'll do as I ask. Now I must go get changed."

He hugged his family tight when he reappeared dressed once more as a Legionnaire.

"Stay safe and come home soon." Marta fought to hold back the tears gathering in her eyes. Klara couldn't and buried her head in her mother's chest.

"I'll send you news as soon as I can." Committing his family's faces to memory, he departed with a cheery wave contradicting his inner anxiety. It might be a long time until he saw them again.

Stefan decided to call on Matous on his way to the assembly point. As he went, he recalled how twenty-four years ago they had both walked together on their way to war, young and naive. It was hard to believe that history was repeating itself and so soon. He consoled himself with the thought that this time he wouldn't be travelling thousands of miles away from home.

Raisa opened the door. She looked dishevelled, strands of hair that was fast turning grey hanging down which she had failed to gather in her bun, her dress smudged with stains from cooking and her eyes red as if she had recently shed tears.

"You're signing up too," she said observing his dress.

"Yes, is Matous?"

"He's in Italy on a concert tour and not due back for a couple of weeks. But Yosef's gone to sign up. Keep an eye on him for me, will you?"

"Of course." Stefan doubted that he would see her son, but Raisa didn't need to know that.

Within twenty-four hours, a million men had joined the Czechoslovak army.

It was with a heavy heart that Stefan returned home only a week later. Britain and France had signed the Munich Agreement and notified

Czechoslovakia that if she fought she would be fighting alone, and so the government had surrendered Sudetenland without a shot being fired. As Chamberlain, the British Prime Minister saw it: "How horrible, fantastic, incredible it is that we should be digging trenches and trying on gas masks here because of a quarrel in a far-away country between people of whom we know nothing."

"Hitler claims he has no more demands," said Stefan to his wife as they lay in bed that night. 'Peace for our time', Chamberlain calls it. But once a wolf has tasted the blood of its prey, he won't stop until he has devoured it all. The government has spent the past few years building fortifications along the border. Now Hitler has them and there's nothing to protect us."

It wasn't many days later when crossing Charles Bridge that Stefan saw his one time friend. Rudi sported a neatly trimmed moustache and beard. He was walking with confidence, almost a swagger, thought Stefan. No doubt recent developments had been to his liking. Stefan was going to look the other way and pretend that he hadn't seen him but Rudi's eyes had already locked on his. Rudi touched the brim of his hat in an ambivalent greeting. Stefan raised his hand slightly and gave a flat smile but Rudi was already looking the other way and marching briskly onwards.

Months passed and it seemed that maybe the wolf had had his fill. The festive season wrapped itself around the city like a welcome cuddle. Candles glowed in windows as if wishing passers by warm greetings.

Marta returned from the market with a carp in a bucket of water to keep it fresh for the main meal on Christmas Eve. On that day, the family breakfasted on vanocka, a Christmas bread-cake, braided with almonds and raisins. In the afternoon, Stefan with Pavel's assistance performed a puppet show in the Old Town Square beneath the massive Christmas tree. This time of year always attracted a large crowd. He would give the money made to one of the charities helping to care for the influx of Czech refugees expelled from Sudetenland.

Come seven, the family sat down to a traditional meal of fish and vegetable soup, followed by fried carp and potato salad, and for dessert little cookies which Klara had decorated. After dinner, Marta placed the metal washbasin filled with water on the table. They each lit a small candle which was inside a walnut shell and placed the four shells on the edge of the bowl. All stayed where they had been put, indicating nothing would change in the coming year save for Pavel's which floated away, signifying he would be leaving.

"Ah, see, Paja," said Marta with pride, "you're

going to get that scholarship and go to university."

Then Marta placed baby Jesus into the bed in the family nativity set, which Stefan's grandfather had carved long ago, and they opened their presents that once the children used to believe Jezisek, little Jesus, had brought.

Midnight mass in St Nicholas that year seemed more magical and the choir more angelic to Stefan than since when he had been a small boy. He could sense the spirit of his parents and his grandparents, recalling how he would squeeze their hands, so excited that it was Christmas, the best time of year.

CHAPTER 19

Early on a March morning in 1939, Stefan awoke to an unfamiliar noise. He glanced at his watch. It was barely gone six. He dressed quietly and slipped out of the apartment to investigate. The morning was grey with light snow swirling.

Outside the sound was more defined, a repeating and disciplined sound but one with a menacing overtone. He hurried down the alleyway to reach Nerudova which led up to the castle. As he did so cold air filled his nostrils and went down his lungs as if he were breathing in a spell cast by the winter witches. People were already assembled, watching mute and gloomy while an unbroken line of soldiers in long coats marched in rows four wide up the hill, rifles on their shoulders and tin helmets on their heads. They weren't Czech soldiers. Stefan's prediction had come to pass, the wolf hadn't been satisfied.

Stefan wondered briefly whether to run home and fetch his rifle but there was no point, it was already too late. Instead, he made his way to Wenceslas Square, the city's focal point and where the inhabitants of Prague gathered for notable events. Tanks stood in position, their turrets rotating with wordless threats. A few spectators had their right arms thrust out and were smiling at the invaders. Some of them threw forget-me-nots and violets, Czechs with German heritage welcoming those that would make them part of the Reich. Most of the crowd, however, were undemonstrative, frozen with disbelief. Stefan had seen enough and departed.

On the way home he noticed German soldiers were already affixing notices with red borders to lamp posts telling people to go about their business as normal. His family were gathered around the radio when he got back to the apartment. He didn't need to tell them what was happening.

The following day, word spread that Hitler had arrived the previous evening and spent the night in the castle, and in the morning briefly appeared on a balcony to a cheering crowd of German Czech students taken up there to do so. A proclamation was issued that Czechs were now part of the Protectorate of Bohemia and Moravia. Slovakia was to be separately administered following its declaration of independence the day before invasion, a move which had been encouraged by the Nazis.

Stefan experienced grief as though he had lost a close friend. His country, a beacon of hope in a world fast descending into a dark abyss, had lasted for a mere twenty years. Only a facade of nationhood remained. President Hacha and his government existed in name rather than substance. The man had been summoned to Berlin the day before the invasion and warned any resistance would be met with overwhelming force and the obliteration of Prague. That fateful night, he had made frantic phone calls to generals not to fight and consequently there had been little resistance by the Czechoslovak army.

In reality everyone knew power now lay with the Reichsprotektor, appointed by Berlin, who would reside in the biggest building of them all, the Cernin Palace located beyond the castle. A colossus at a hundred and fifty metres in length with Palladian columns, it dwarfed the pretty Loreta church opposite with her white towers and onion-domes, and shouted out domination. A lair for the beasts who would control the city, clicking their heels together and dictating who should live and who should die.

Once again German became the official language and German street signs returned. The Vltava, the riverine artery of the country, was renamed the Moldau. German Czechs became citizens of the Reich. Other Czechs would become mere cogs in Germany's juggernaut, producing weapons in their factories for the Nazi war machine.

An ominous quiet descended over the city and the bells of Prague ceased to chime. They had been taken away to be melted down to make armaments for the occupiers.

A quiet fell over the apartment also. Only a short

while after the invasion, Marta thrust a note into Stefan's hand immediately he opened the front door.

"Read this." She half suppressed a sob.

Pavel had left. He was going to try and make his way to England and offer his services to the Czechoslovak government in exile headed by former President Benes in London.

"What we witnessed on Christmas Eve wasn't him going to university. I'm so worried about what might happen to him," said Marta.

"It's probably a good thing. Who knows what the Germans will do with our young men who stay here. Maybe send them to Germany to do forced labour or fight for them. We should be happy that he's gone somewhere safe."

"Safe? How do we know that? He could be arrested before he gets there. And what if there's a war between Britain and Germany?"

"We should hope that there is. Unless France and Britain or the Soviet Union take up arms and defeat Hitler how will we ever be free again?"

Marta flopped onto a dining chair like a rag doll.

"I'll miss him so. He was noisy and messy, infuriating at times, but he brought life and laughter."

"Me too. How's Klara taking it?"

"Upset, of course. You know how she adores her older brother, always has. She's followed him around like a puppy since she could walk. She'll be lost without him."

When Stefan next saw Matous, he had a similar story.

"Yosef has left too, gone to Poland to get to Russia. We can't blame them. At their age we would have done the same. Come to think of it we did, fighting for the Legion, though the Austro-Hungarian Empire was a lot more benign than the crazy people in Berlin. I don't understand how they can be so full of hatred."

"Have you thought about what you'll do given how they've treated the Jews in Germany?"

"Radka has suggested getting false papers for me and the children, and the four of us taking a trip to Poland and then heading to England or America. But I can't leave Raisa behind, and the children wouldn't go without her. I've heard about an English organisation that is able to get visas for children if they can find a family in England willing to take them. Jakub's probably too old to be accepted but Sarinka should be."

The organisation was led by an English banker, Nicholas Winton. He would arrange for over six hundred Jewish children to be sent by train from Prague to England and safety.

"Oh, Matous, that would be so hard for you. What does Raisa say?"

"I'm waiting for the right moment to ask her. Every time I'm about too I can't do it - can't believe that I'm suggesting sending our little girl away to a foreign country and maybe never seeing her again." Matous swallowed hard. "But I know we must do whatever we can to make Sarinka safe even though it'll break our hearts."

"These are indeed terrible times."

"The Soviets would have saved us if the Poles had allowed them to cross their land to get here."

"You're still a communist then," commented Stefan.

"Even more so now. Look at the French and British, they didn't lift a finger to help us. They're part of the old order. A Europe for the rich, not the workers."

"You'd better keep those thoughts to yourself. They say the first thing the Nazis did was to arrest all prominent Czech communists."

"I know. Say, do you and Marta want to come to the National next week. We're doing a concert, Smetana's 'My country', a chance for us to show that they can't kill what we believe in. I can get you some free tickets. You can sit with Raisa and keep her company."

"Yes, Marta would love it."

The National Theatre epitomised the Czech spirit. Built from donations given by ordinary Czechs towards the end of the nineteenth century, it stands by the banks of the Vltava, distinctive with its external sky blue roof marked with stars and crested in gold. The interior is an explosion of red and gold and the ceiling is adorned with frescoes.

While waiting for the performance to start Raisa

spoke of the plan she and Matous had now discussed to send Sara to England, tears coursing freely down her cheeks as she did so.

"Am I a bad mother, Marta, not wanting her to go?"

"No, of course not. I'd feel exactly the same. If I'd known of Paja's intentions, I would have done my utmost to stop him."

"But if I don't send her and something happens to her, how could I ever forgive myself knowing that she could have been safe? It's hard enough Yosef having gone off to war, but he's an adult and speaks fluent Russian. Sarinka can't speak a word of English. She'll be so alone, so lonely."

"Have you mentioned it to her?"

"No, how can you explain to a six year old that you're sending her away to a foreign country to live with strangers. If she goes, I'll probably lie and say we'll all be following soon."

Marta took Raisa's hand in hers. "I wish I could give you an answer but only you and Matous can decide. It wouldn't be forever. One day this nightmare will end and we'll all wake up to a brand new day."

Clapping for the arrival on stage of the orchestra and conductor, Vaclav Talich, interrupted their conversation. The women were dressed in elegant long black dresses, the men in dinner jackets and dress shirts.

Marta knew about Radmila, Stefan had told her. She saw Raisa's eyes darting around and fixing

on a woman with a violin. It was obvious that
Raisa knew too. Marta never saw her once look
at Matous. Each time she glanced at her friend,
Raisa was still fixated on her rival. It was hard to
see Radmila clearly from the distance they were,
but Marta could tell she was thin and most probably glamorous, not a woman who had given
birth three times and was worn down from a
life of cooking and cleaning from morning until
night.

The evening was as defiant an expression of
Czech identity as was possible under their new
rulers. The audience's response to the patriotic
music was ecstatic and culminated in a spontaneous outburst of the Czechoslovak national anthem. It wasn't long afterwards until the Nazi's
restricted what could be played, outlawing much
of that music.

CHAPTER 20

"Where's Klara?" Stefan asked his wife when he came upstairs, tired after another long day in his workshop. "She always seems to be out these days."

"Out with friends. It's summer after all, and we can't begrudge her some pleasure. There's not enough happiness in the times we're living through."

"There's something I need to tell you."

Stefan said the words with great seriousness and Marta felt her mouth go dry. She knew how men got tired of their wives. It had happened to Raisa. Marta had often thought about it happening to her and now it seemed the time had arrived.

"I've joined the resistance."

"Oh." Marta didn't react initially, that wasn't what she had been expecting to hear.

"I've agreed to move guns and ammunition around the city in my puppet theatre. No one's going to suspect what I'm up to."

"I certainly hope so. When will all this start?"

"It already has."

"Do be careful, Stefan. This isn't just about our

lives. Klara will suffer too if you're caught."

"I won't be. I'll skip dinner tonight, I've a delivery to make."

"But-"

Stefan put his arms around Marta and gave her a hug. "Don't you worry. I'll be back in a couple of hours."

Stefan had been approached a few weeks earlier by the man who supplied him with wood. Bringing a delivery to Stefan's workshop, the two of them had discussed the occupation. They had known each other a long time and trusted each other enough to be quite open.

"Have you ever thought about helping?"

"I'd love too," Stefan had answered. "But what can I do, a mere puppeteer? I suppose I could create a puppet of Hitler and make him look stupid in my shows, but what will that achieve except getting me arrested?"

"My timber yard's become a storage point for guns and ammunition being smuggled into the city. I was wondering if you'd be willing to help distribute them. I've twice had my vehicle stopped and searched. Luckily, I wasn't transporting any but the next time I could be. You're much less likely to be stopped pushing your puppet theatre around, and if you see there's a check point up ahead, it's easy for you to divert down an alleyway. Would you think about it?"

"I don't need to think about it. When do you want me to start?"

The man was right, whenever Stefan saw soldiers or police he disappeared down another street. He knew the city like the back of his hand. Soon he was out making deliveries once or twice a week.

While Stefan might be weary nearly all the time, he got to put his feet up each evening and smoke his pipe after eating a dinner Marta had cooked for him. His own son was in a foreign country with no one to look after him and risking his young life in the war effort. It made Stefan feel better about himself that he was finally doing something too.

In Letna Park, Klara was strolling along the leafy pathways arm in arm with a young man. The evening sunshine caught her face in its golden glow, accentuating her ripening beauty. They stopped at the lookout point above the Vltava which gave a fine view of its bridges, and beyond the roofs of Prague releasing the warmth of the day. He put his arm around her and they kissed.

The couple had met several weeks earlier. Klara had been browsing in a bookshop. When she left, a young man had come chasing after her with money she had dropped. She'd thanked him and they'd chatted for a while, discovering that they both loved books. When he'd suggested they meet for coffee she hadn't hesitated. His wide smile and sultry eyes had been irresistible.

She found him so easy to talk to, a kindred

spirit, and one who told her she should pursue her dream of studying literature. Klara had never found the support she'd hoped for from her parents. Talk of university had always been directed towards Pavel. Her mother had suggested training to be a teacher as if that was the only suitable career for a woman with academic interests.

Feeling lost when her brother left and without even confiding in her, Klara's new friend helped fill the empty space in her heart. They had been on several dates already, to the cinema, cafes, even a subterranean jazz club where the beat bounced off the walls. It seemed so terribly modern and exciting to Klara.

She hadn't told her parents about her boyfriend yet, her father was so anti-German. But it wasn't Jürgen's fault that Hitler had invaded. Jürgen might be a German Czech but he had lived in Prague his entire life.

The sun had become a large orange ball, visibly sinking behind the castle on the hill above Mala Strana when Stefan pushed his puppet theatre into his workshop, another delivery safely made. He had adapted the lower half of the back of his theatre on wheels, inserting internal partitions on either side which it was hard to see were there, except on close examination. They could hold a gun or two or several grenades and many bullets.

He shut the door and sat down on his stool,

exhausted from the fear of being apprehended whenever he was out. A knock on the door startled him. No one ever came to his workshop other than Marta, and she never bothered knocking. Cautiously, he opened the door a few centimetres.

"Hello, Stefan."

His mouth dropped open faster than a falling guillotine. He ushered in his visitor, closing the door quickly.

"Dagmar, what are you doing here?"

"I'm sorry to bother you but I've run out of hiding places."

"Hiding places?"

"The Nazis issued a warrant for my arrest and several other members of Parliament that they consider too left wing. I hid at my parents for a night but it seemed obvious they'd come looking for me there, and since then a couple of friends have housed me. I've run out of options. I was hoping maybe I could stay with you. Only for a while," she quickly added, noting the consternation on Stefan's face.

"I'm not sure Marta would-"

"I don't mean in your apartment. I can stay down here in your workshop."

Stefan scratched the top of his head. He was conflicted. If he told Marta, she would likely be against it. She was already unhappy enough about his gun running activities, let alone giving refuge to someone the Germans wanted, and someone he had once dated. Yet he needed to help Dagmar, her life was in danger, it was his patriotic duty. Many other public figures had already been captured. "All right."

"Thank you, Stefan." Dagmar threw her arms around him in relief and gratitude. It reminded Stefan of when they had been young and close. Dagmar's hug was, however, short lived.

"I'd say make yourself comfortable but there's nothing to sit on apart from my stool and nothing to lie on."

"I don't care, it's a whole lot better than a Nazi prison would be."

That night when Marta was asleep Stefan crept out of bed, wincing each time one of the floorboards creaked in case she should wake. Taking a blanket from the cupboard and some food and water, he tiptoed down the flights of stairs.

Stefan observed Dagmar as she ate. She was still as beautiful as she had always been. He wondered if she had really meant what she said the last time they had met, or whether that had been what she had felt obliged to say to get him to leave her alone. Didn't the invasion change everything? Who knew whether they would still be alive next year, or even next week?

CHAPTER 21

Stefan spent the greatest part of his waking hours in his workshop, he always had. Now that meant he spent most of his time with Dagmar. Disinterested in books himself, he nonetheless brought down ones belonging to Marta for Dagmar. He knew the days must seem interminably long to her.

He enjoyed their time together. They didn't talk often, yet just being in her presence made him feel content, she reading while he carved and chiselled.

"I saw Rudi once a while back, crossing the Charles Bridge but we didn't speak," he commented.

"He remarried, I was pleased for him. He has two children now."

Stefan bristled, he still felt resentment towards Rudi. Stefan had persuaded himself long ago that Dagmar would have been married to him if only Rudi had married someone else the first time around.

When Marta went out shopping, Stefan would take Dagmar up to the apartment so that she could wash herself and rinse out her clothes. She had arrived with only a small bag.

"You have beautiful children," said Dagmar admiring the photograph on the dresser. "You must worry about Pavel."

"I do, we've heard nothing from him. And as for Klara, I don't see much of her. She's out most of the time. We're worried she'll be sent away to work in one of the factories, making planes or tanks for the Germans."

"I'm sure a big reason for invading us was exactly that. Czechoslovakia had a thriving armaments industry, perfect for keeping the Nazis supplied if they decide to start a war which I'm sure they will before long."

"Well, let's hope someone does or you'll be stuck here in this workshop with me for ever," joked Stefan.

"I really do appreciate all you're doing for me."

"I'm glad to do so. It's the brave people like you who keep our flame of freedom alive."

"A freedom you helped create when you fought in Russia. I'm sorry for the hurt I caused you back then."

Their conversation ended but as they stood there their eyes still spoke to each other. An overpowering urge surged through Stefan. He placed his palms gently on Dagmar's cheeks and his lips on hers. She didn't resist. Initial kisses of tenderness exploded into an intense passion that neither wanted to control. Back in the workshop,

Stefan held her tight and close.

After that day, their long silences had an intimacy which they hadn't before and the workshop became their love nest. There was an edge, always present, that the Nazis might come knocking. The danger of discovery added an excitement and urgency to their relationship. Stefan's life had become crazy, reckless, carrying weapons across the city and starting an affair. Yet it made the adrenaline flow and gave him a rush he found addictive. He couldn't fight the feeling or maybe it was that he didn't want to. Middle age was no longer predictable and mundane. It was as if he had managed to reclaim the thrill of youth. It reminded him of how exciting life had once been.

When once they heard Marta's footsteps on the stairs, Dagmar quickly grabbed her things and hid in the cupboard.

Life was becoming increasingly difficult for Matous and Raisa. New ordinances had been issued limiting the access of Jews to public places. They were banned from restaurants and cafes. Jewish residences had to be registered and radios handed in. Stefan and Matous could no longer meet in bars for drinks so Stefan visited Matous' apartment. He hadn't expected to see his mother open the door.

"The Nazis took our home," explained Mrs Rubinstein observing his look of surprise at her presence. As always, she was impeccably dressed in fine clothes and her three gold chains which hung from her neck and almost reached her waist. She seemed out of place in this apartment where damp caused the faded wallpaper to peel off, revealing the mould underneath.

Matous' father was seated in an armchair in the corner of the room. Slouched and clearly demoralised, he barely muttered a greeting. Stefan sensed from the quick eye roll Raisa gave him as she looked up from her knitting that relations with the in-laws weren't much improved even though, and probably because, they now shared a home, and a very confined one.

"Let's go in the kitchen," said Matous. It was only a narrow galley, but a place where they could talk without being listened to. "I feel for my parents. After what they're used to, it's one hell of a come down but having them here is difficult. Mother spends a lot of the time crying, railing against their misfortune, and my father hardly utters a word all day long. He was fired from his job at the bank which has really hit him hard. He was one of Prague's pre-eminent bankers. He's a lost soul."

"You and Raisa will have to come for dinner. In fact spend as much time at our place as you want and come whenever you like."

"That's kind, thank you. I think we'll take you up on that offer."

"What about the orchestra, is your own job safe?"

"For now, but for how long I don't know."

"Tatka, I'm hungry." Sara had run into the kitchen, her big hazel eyes endearing as a puppy's.

"In a minute. Go play for a while." Sara stamped one of her feet with frustration and departed.

"She asks me why the Rabbis can't protect us from the Nazis. Why they can't create another Golem from the mud in the Vltava as in the legend from hundreds of years ago when a Rabbi is said to have done so and made a huge, vaguely human looking creature to protect the Jewish quarter. That is until Golem ran amok and turned on his master and had to be locked away." Matous' expression became solemn. "Raisa's finally agreed to sending Sarinka to England. We're hoping to get her on a train planned for September." His voice cracked with emotion.

Stefan felt almost guilty that he didn't have to face such a terrible choice. He abandoned his intention to tell Matous about Dagmar. Such news seemed self-absorbed by comparison.

That evening, Klara was late home for dinner yet again.

"What time do you call this?" demanded Stefan.

She quickly took her seat to join her parents at the table. "I'm sorry, I lost track of time."

Stefan wasn't placated. "Sorry's not good enough. Where exactly have you been? I've had enough of my daughter running around the city like a...like a..." He held back from saying the word that sprang to mind.

His wife adopted a more conciliatory approach. "We're only concerned for your welfare. Things are dangerous right now. Do you understand why we worry?"

"You don't need to. I spend my time with someone who would always keep me safe."

"Someone?" Marta gave a mischievous smile. "Who is this someone? We should meet him to put our minds at ease."

"He's twenty years old. Kind, intelligent, and from a good family."

"What does he do?" asked Stefan.

"He works for the police."

"Police," repeated Stefan. "Well, that doesn't make me happy. They're Nazi stooges, enforcing their rules."

"Stefan." Marta reached out and touched his arm, trying to defuse the situation. "What's his name? "Jürgen."

"Jürgen!" spat out Stefan as if his daughter had uttered a profanity. "You mean he's German?"

"No, he's Czech, born and raised in Prague like me."

"No, he's a German Czech. The very same people who conspired with Hitler to invade our country. The people who welcomed the Nazis with open arms." Stefan's voice had risen with anger.

"He's not a Nazi, he's not interested in politics."

"He's not one of us that's for sure, he's with the enemy. Your own brother is risking his life to free our country, Matous and Raisa and their family face persecution, and yet you, my own daughter, is cavorting with one of those who would hurt our family and friends." Stefan's face had reddened and the vein in his forehead was pulsating.

"I'm not cavorting," protested Klara. "We're in love."

"In love," scoffed Stefan. "You know nothing about it. I forbid you ever to see him again."

Klara pushed her chair back and stood up. "You don't understand. What's happening isn't his fault, you can't keep us apart."

Stefan brought his fist down hard on the table. "You will obey me or you can get out of my home."

Klara ran off to her room.

"Why did you have to be so inflexible," accused Marta. "You haven't even met him."

"What? So you think we should welcome the enemy into our family. If you don't agree with me, just consider what your son would think."

"I agree it's not what we want for her, but pushing her into a corner is only likely to drive her into his arms."

Stefan grunted. They ate the rest of their meal in silence.

"I'm going down to the workshop. I have things to finish off. Don't bother waiting up, I'll be some while."

CHAPTER 22

It wasn't many days later that Marta greeted Stefan with a tear stained face.

"Klara's gone, she's left a note. She's getting married tomorrow."

Stefan bit his lip and squeezed his eyes shut, fighting the feelings inside of him which wanted to express themselves. Klarinka, his sweet little girl who had grown up so fast, the apple of his eye, had gone, run away. Her footsteps would no longer echo around the apartment or her laughter lift him up from the bleakness of today's world.

"I'm going to the wedding, she's still our daughter," said Marta. "I hope you will come too."

But Stefan didn't.

Klara and Jürgen had a civil ceremony. They married in the Old Town Hall. A large swastika hung from its exterior. Marta arrived moments before the start. She hadn't known what to wear, putting on her best dress and then taking it off before deciding to wear it. She was relieved that Stefan had stayed down in his workshop which had avoided another argument about her attendance.

As she sat down Marta dabbed her eyes, thinking of how this was about as far as possible from how she thought her daughter's wedding day would be. Klara wore a pale blue dress, not the white one with a long train her mother had always envisaged. There was no choir, no music, and no real sense of occasion. But Marta could see true love in the couple's eyes when they looked at each other. Mother and daughter exchanged no words, only a wistful half smile. When the ceremony ended and Jürgen's family gathered around the bride and groom to congratulate them, Marta slipped away. Outside she let her feelings flow as she wound her way through the familiar but now unfriendly streets of Prague.

Stefan didn't ask her about the wedding and she didn't tell him about it.

Marta was grateful that she had found many wanting private tuition, allowing her to bury herself in her work for at least part of her days. When she wasn't busy, free time taunted her, poking her heart with worries about her son and her daughter.

Soon there was another worry to occupy Marta's mind. Her career as a teacher had taught her to have eyes in the back of her head and to be capable of sniffing out when something wasn't quite right better than a hound with his nose to the ground. Her books out of order on her book-shelf, soapy suds left on the floor, pieces of food disappearing, Marta had put such matters down to Klara. She was a disorganised teenager after all and loved to snack between meals. Yet that couldn't be the reason, not any longer.

"What's going on, Stefan?" she asked as they sat drinking their after dinner coffee, now much weaker than she used to make it to stretch out the small amount remaining for as long as possible.

"Going on? I don't know what you mean."

"Oh, I think you do," said Marta in her most school mistress like of tones. "You never read books, and I've never once seen you wash anything, yet…" She didn't finish her sentence letting the last word hang in the space between them like a spotlight shining on her husband.

Stefan became uncomfortably hot and wondered if it showed.

"Well?" Her eyes wouldn't let his go. He was trapped, and the manacles were tightening. There was no choice but to confess.

"I've been hiding something from you… I didn't want to add to your worries. I've given refuge to someone the Nazis are after. She's hiding in the workshop. Dagmar Danekova, the member of Parliament."

"How did she end up here?" Marta's heart had begun beating like a drum but she willed herself to appear as calm as a lake on a day without a breath of wind.

"She'd run out of places to go. She turned up a couple of weeks back."

"A couple?" Marta had noticed misplaced books and soap suds on the floor well before that.

"A month maybe, I don't remember."

Marta said nothing for a moment as she thought about how to deal with the situation. Stefan waited for her rebuke but her eyes didn't fill with anger.

"Well, we can't have the woman living down there, it must be so uncomfortable. Go fetch her. She can have Klara's room, and I'd welcome the company."

"But I thought you'd be angry, cross that I was putting us in danger."

"You were already doing enough to get us both arrested if you were ever caught. You did the right thing, we need to help those we can. Our son's already risking his life wherever he is and whatever he's doing. When we get to the end of our lives, do we want to look back in pride or in shame?"

Stefan was lost for words. He had never expected her reaction to be so sanguine. Dagmar, however, understood immediately but didn't share her conclusion with him.

"I really appreciate your kindness," said Dagmar when she came up with Stefan.

"It's the least we can do to help in the fight. I can't believe Stefan has kept you down in that dusty old workshop. And even at the best of times, he's not a conversationalist. You must have been bored to distraction."

The first morning when Stefan went down to his workshop and Dagmar was left alone with Marta, Dagmar felt pricks of guilty perspiration break out all over her the instant he had gone.

"Were you not lonely pursuing a career?" asked Marta as she washed the breakfast things and Dagmar stood beside her, drying them with a tea towel.

"No, it was fulfilling. Maybe when I'm old and grey I might regret not having a family, but I don't believe it should have to be a choice. Women should have the opportunities men do if they want them."

"I'd agree with you there. I miss teaching a class of children."

"Exactly. Why must all other avenues close if we marry. And our divorce laws are so restrictive. So many women are trapped in unhappy marriages, and if they leave they get nothing."

"Indeed, even if their husbands commit adultery."

Dagmar felt herself blush and quickly changed the topic of conversation. "What can I do around the house to help? Maybe with me here, you can have more time for yourself."

It wasn't too long until Stefan also understood Marta's motives for wanting Dagmar in the apartment. Marta went out as little as she could, and when she had to, said she would only be gone for a short while.

Dagmar rejected the advances Stefan tried to make in his wife's absence. "It's over, Stefan. And it's for the best."

"But I love you."

"No, you don't. You love the thrill, the excitement. It wouldn't have lasted, and it's not worth wrecking your marriage for. You should count yourself lucky, Marta must really love you. I should move on."

"But you've got nowhere to go. Stay."

They spoke rarely after that and avoided each other's gaze even though it was too late to hide their secret. Stefan came to loathe himself for what he had done. Marta deserved so much better. She had been a good wife, it was he who had fallen short.

When Raisa and Matous came for dinner, Matous' expression was as startled as if Radmila had been sitting at the table.

"I believe you two already know each other," said Marta, a hint of enjoyment in her voice at his obvious awkwardness.

"Yes, from long ago, before the last war. How are you Dagmar?"

"Well, thank you, apart from having to hide from the Nazis. Marta and Stefan have kindly taken me in. Hello, you must be Raisa. It's so nice to meet you."

When they sat down to eat, Stefan sought to steer the conversation in a different direction. "How is everything with the family?"

"It's not easy," said Raisa, "but we're coping."

"At least now France and England have declared war on Germany, there could be light at the end of the tunnel for all of us," said Dagmar.

"Too bad they didn't do that when Hitler seized Sudetenland, or invaded the rest of our country. They just gave him longer to get stronger," commented Stefan.

"I hope you're right, Dagmar. Things get worse for us every single day," said Matous.

"What about Sarinka?" Marta asked Raisa.

Raisa's shoulder muscles tightened and her mind travelled back to that awful morning.

The sun had been so bright, the sky brilliant, a day that seemed to defy sadness, yet her heart ached so much she thought it would rupture as she and Matous walked Sara to the station, each tightly holding one of her precious little hands, the last time that they might ever do so. Raisa wanted to weep, to scream in despair, but she couldn't, not in front of her daughter. They had told Sara they would be joining her soon, that England was to be their new home where there were no Nazis, only friendly people.

On the station platform two hundred and fifty other children, from tiny tots to teenagers, stood with their parents, some curious, some bewildered, some crying. The sight of so many families about to be broken up and smashed by the hammer of hate made Raisa feel dizzy. She reached out for the wall and leaned against it.

They waited and waited for the train. Each time Raisa heard that chugging noise and saw that belching black smoke approach, she wanted to grab Sara and run, and each time a train pulled in and it wasn't theirs was a slow torture knowing that another one would soon follow. It was gone noon when the station manager came along the platform gesticulating with his hands and telling people to leave. The train's been cancelled, go home, he'd said. Raisa hadn't been able to contain her emotion any longer and wrapped Sara in her arms, sobbing with relief.

"The war has put paid to our plans to send Sarinka to England. The train was due to leave the day Hitler invaded Poland," explained Matous.

"Oh, I am sorry," sympathised Marta.

"At least we'll all be staying together," said Raisa. Marta observed that Raisa didn't look disappointed that Sara hadn't been able to leave Prague which was understandable. The dilemma of what to do for the best no longer existed. The choice had been made for her, but would she come to regret what she may well have wished for.

"I hear you're a Communist," Dagmar said to Matous.

"Yes. With respect, Social Democrats like you will

never be able to change people's lives the way you'd like too."

"And Communists will? Aren't you upset that the Soviets made a deal with Hitler and carved up Poland with him?"

"That was a surprise, I grant you. Stalin has a long term strategy, I'm quite sure of it. A conflict between Russia and Germany is unavoidable, one a force for good, the other unadulterated evil."

"Politics." Marta pronounced the word with disdain. "Isn't there something lighter we can talk about. I swear you'll give me indigestion if you carry on."

"I'm envious of Raisa," said Marta as she and Stefan lay in bed that night. "She has two of her children at home. We've lost both of ours."

"Paja's not lost, he's away fighting for us. As for Klara, hopefully as this war progresses, she'll realise the mistake she has made. You shouldn't envy Raisa. The laws against the Jews are getting worse all the time. Who knows what will happen to them if this war doesn't end soon, and with Germany's defeat."

"We should hide them here if they find themselves in danger."

"We don't have room for all of them, let alone enough to feed them, and the neighbours would be bound to notice something."

"Well, what about Sara? We could take her in."

"I'll talk to Matous about it. You're a good

woman, Marta. I'm sorry I let you down."

"People have worse to cope with than I do." She rolled over away from Stefan and turned off the bedside lamp. In the darkness, she lay awake a long time thinking of what she might do when the war was over. Her children were grown and she could put herself first for a change. Not since she was a teenager had she enjoyed that luxury. Even before her marriage there had been her father to cook and clean for when her mother died. A school was unlikely to accept a woman divorced or separated from her husband as a teacher, but private tuition could provide enough for her to live on. She needn't tell clients her true circumstances. If pressed, she could declare herself a widow. She would ponder on it further, she decided.

The shouting and heavy footfalls on the staircase at daybreak the following morning woke them both with a start.

CHAPTER 23

"I'll check this one. You go check the top one." The command from the floor below was given in German. Marta and Stefan ran out of their bedroom at the same time as Dagmar emerged from Klara's room. The front door to the apartment was unlocked and flew open before they could do anything. Stefan's legs became as soft as jelly and he felt like he'd been lassoed. Their papers would be demanded, their identities checked. Dagmar would be taken away, and he and Marta too for sheltering her. Would it be prison or execution? They would search his workshop and they would find the guns. He broke out in a cold sweat, it would be execution.

The soldier saw the three of them, cornered and guilty looking. He went to raise his rifle and opened his mouth as if about to shout for his colleagues but he didn't. His surprise was as great as two of his quarry.

"Rudi." Dagmar pronounced his name so quietly that it was barely audible. The facial hair had gone, he was in the Wehrmacht now.

He said not a word looking from Dagmar to

Stefan and back, stoney faced and giving no hint of his intentions. The moment froze and time stopped. Then he reacted, he turned to shout. Marta let out a moan of despair.

"All is in order up here."

He departed without even glancing at them again, slamming the door behind him. Marta and Dagmar embraced each other, unable to believe their good fortune.

Marta made the last of the coffee she had, and they sat around the table in their nightclothes still in a state of shock. Stefan had to fight to steady his hand as he raised his cup to his lips.

"Was that your old friend?" Marta asked Stefan.

"Yes. He, Matous and I were such good friends until we got sent off to fight. He didn't believe in our new country, feared that Germans would be discriminated against and now he's got his wish."

"Rudi," repeated Marta as the cogs of her mind turned. "And how did you know him, Dagmar? He clearly recognised you."

"We... we were married for a short while just after the last war."

"Oh." Marta said the word casually as if it was of no consequence to conceal her surprise.

"I'll pack my things and leave tonight."

"You don't need to do that," said Marta. "They've already searched us."

"No, it's too dangerous for you both for me to remain here. They could be back, and it won't be Rudi next time. I'm forever grateful for what you've done for me. I'll be all right, really I will."

"Where will you go?"

"I'll walk out into the country. I have an aunt and uncle about twenty kilometres outside the city."

Marta thought she probably wasn't telling the truth but didn't pursue the matter. Late that evening Marta and Stefan peered out of the window, watching Dagmar disappear into the fickle arms of the night.

"I couldn't help but like her," commented Marta. "I really hope she survives and is able to carry on her good work once this nightmare is over. I admire what she's done and what she stands for. There were precious few in our Parliament who had the courage to speak out as she did, especially when it came to women's rights."

"It's nature's way, a man provides and a woman raises the family and keeps the home."

"Nature's way," she repeated contemptuously. "You mean it's what men want. I'm going to bed."

Marta lay awake unpicking the day's events and her new window into the past. She knew her husband and Dagmar had dated when they were young. He had told her, said it had meant nothing. But was his recent fling with her more than that? Had he wanted to marry Dagmar all along but Rudi had got back to Prague first and won the prize? Marta wondered if Stefan had ever loved her, had he always been in love with Dagmar? She had thought he was one of those undemonstrative men who found it difficult to show affection. When Stefan opened the bedroom door she shut her eyes and pretended to be asleep.

Christmas 1939 was more different to last year's than the couple could possibly have imagined twelve months ago. The jagged hole in their lives created by their children's departure was particularly sharp that day. Rationing had been introduced and many things were unobtainable. Not that either really cared. The meal on Christmas Eve had none of the pleasure it used to bring without their son and daughter to share it with. Stefan experienced no magic as he had at last year's midnight mass. The church seemed cold and unwelcoming, the congregation subdued and preoccupied. And there were no longer any bells to ring out the hope of the season. It was as if God himself had abandoned Prague.

The day after Christmas a snow flurry had coated the roof tops like icing sugar. However, a steel sky made the city appear sullen. The witches had returned and were in full control.

"I'm going for a walk, I want some fresh air," announced Marta.

"Would you like me to come along?"

"No, I need some time alone."

Marta hid the gift which she had under her coat. She caught a tram and got off by Charles University. That there had been both a German and a Czech university even before the Nazis came, spoke volumes about the country's longstanding divisions. The Czech one had been closed after students had protested at the funeral of a fellow student who had died from wounds after being shot by the authorities at demonstrations against the occupation on Czechoslovakia's national day in October. That day citizens had boycotted the trams because they announced stops in German, and in Wenceslas Square and the Old Town Square hundreds had gathered and tore down German signs until the police opened fire. The funeral protests had seen many arrested with nine students executed and twelve hundred sent off to a concentration camp.

Marta shuddered as she remembered. Pavel could have been a protestor too if he hadn't gone to England. Gone, but had he got there? He had never written, or maybe he had and his letters had been intercepted. Was he still alive even? Not knowing was like a knife to the chest which stabbed her daily.

Two streets farther on, Marta reached their building. She climbed the stairs and knocked. There was no sound from within. Marta left her small parcel outside their door. 'To Klara and Jürgen' said the label.

The New Year ushered in greater oppression, particularly for the Jews. The places they could go became ever fewer in number and their children were expelled from state schools.

When Raisa and Matous visited Marta and Stefan's the news was bleak.

"They've taken down Mendelssohn's statue from the Rudolfinum. You can't have a Jew standing with such musical greats as Mozart, can you?" said Matous with sarcasm. "And I've been expelled from the orchestra. At least I won't have to sit on a stage festooned with swastikas and look out at the rows of self righteous Nazis sitting there as if they were cultured, upstanding members of society."

"Do you have enough to live on?" asked Stefan.

"Yes, father still has his money until they steal if off him which I expect they will before long. In any event, there's not a lot to buy. We Jews can only go food shopping between three and four when most of what is available has already been sold, and we can't visit clothes shops anymore. We are supposed to buy what we need from the junk shops. Mother swears she'll dress in bedsheets before she will get her clothes from such places."

"If you let me know what you want, I can go buy things for you," said Marta.

"My dear, Marta, what would we do without you, without either of you," said Raisa.

Marta took that as her cue to raise the matter.

"Stefan and I have been talking. We've been thinking about Sarinka. If things should get worse, we wanted you to know that we could take her in and keep her safe until you are able to have her back. And with me being a teacher, I can ensure that her education isn't interrupted."

Raisa's eyes filled with emotion. "That is beyond kind, but I can't see the authorities accepting that our daughter has magically disappeared. They know where we live and who our family members are. They'd probably torture us until we confessed, and then you would be at risk."

"Unless they have reason to believe that she's dead. I know of someone who might be able to forge a death certificate," said Matous.

"Let's hope things don't get to that point, but if they do our offer is open," said Stefan.

"We would pay you of course," said Raisa who, contrary to Marta thinking she might not like the idea, seemed to be in favour.

"You will do no such thing," objected Marta. "We have plenty, and having Sarinka's company would be reward enough. My private tuition business is growing all the time, and what with that and the money Stefan makes we have more than we need."

She hadn't told Stefan that most of her pupils were the children of German Czechs, and that some were even the children of German military personnel stationed in the city.

Stefan carried on making puppets and doing shows. He also continued with his gun running. Neither the Protectorate Police nor the Nazis ever stopped him. Never, until one day they did.

CHAPTER 24

Stefan pushed his theatre across the Old Town Square. They'd put up a giant picture of Hitler, an ugly blot on the Squares' beauty like those Nazi flags. He ignored them and went down Celetna. Not far now to his drop off point. Stefan went under the arch of the imposing fifty metre high medieval Powder Gate, the last survivor of the thirteen towers which formed part of the wall that had once protected the Old Town. Its surface was black with the soot of centuries, giving it a foreboding appearance in current circumstances.

"Hey, puppeteer." The shout came from two men standing by the far side of the archway who had been outside of Stefan's field of vision as he came through it. Their uniforms like the tower were also black and foreboding, members of the SS. Stefan's nonchalance was replaced by fear. "Give us a show."

"I'm in a hurry."

"I said give us a show." The man had menace in his eyes.

Stefan positioned his theatre so that he was behind it. Did they really want a show or was this an unsubtle prelude to a search, he wondered.

Stefan bent down, opening the small doors to where his puppets were kept. As he did so a couple of bullets fell out onto the ground. He put out his hand to catch them but he wasn't quick enough. They rolled past his theatre and into full view, only coming to a stop after a couple of metres. Stefan expected the men to rush around and grab him, ripping his theatre apart while they searched for more. Fortunately they had been absorbed in conversation with each other.

"Get on with it!" barked the other one.

Stefan opened the stage curtains. Holding the strings of a puppet in each hand, he made them dance. His co-ordination was off, his mind captured by the demon bullets which had escaped and were begging for attention. Out of the corner of his eye, he saw a young boy approach and deftly kneel, pretending to tie his shoe lace as he scooped up his treasure. Stefan exhaled, it had been a close shave. He reprimanded himself. In future, he wouldn't be so careless and check nothing was ever loose like that again. This wasn't a game of hide and seek, it was a matter of life and death.

"I've had enough of this Czech peasant shit," announced one of the SS. "Come on, let's go." With relief, Stefan watched the men depart.

As the months passed, rations were cut and

everyday items such as soap, tobacco, shoes and clothes became hard to find. News of how the war might really be going was hard to come by. Even the Prager Tagblatt, the newspaper Rudi had once worked for and which had slavishly praised the Nazis after the invasion, had been shut down. Most Czechs boycotted the Nazi newspaper, Der Neue Tag, The New Day. Radio also spewed out their propaganda. If the endless claims of German victories were true, prospects of Czechoslovakia regaining its freedom were remote. A weary resignation settled on the populace. People got by as best they could. There was nothing else they could do. If they rose up they would be slaughtered.

Matters took a turn for the worse in the autumn of 1941 when Rheinhard Heydrich became the Reichsprotektor. Nicknamed "Billy Goat" by his peers at naval college, the man had a falsetto voice. Dishonourably discharged as a young man from the navy, he delighted in the vengeance and hatred of the Nazi regime and had risen fast within its ranks. He viewed Czechs as vermin and Jews as worse. They were required to wear a yellow star whenever in public, making them even easier targets for abuse by the Nazis, and those Czechs who were anti-Semitic, of which there were many.

It was a stormy late November afternoon and almost dark when Matous and Sara arrived at the apartment soaking wet, their hair plastered to their scalps and their coats dripping water onto the floor and creating small puddles.

"Dry off by the fire while I get you a hot drink and something to eat," said Marta who couldn't help but notice that Matous was carrying a small suitcase.

"It's time," he said. "They've started moving those Jews who don't already live there into Josefov, and there's rumours they're going to start moving people somewhere else before long."

Marta kneeled down before Sara who wore a forlorn expression and took the girl's hands in hers.

"Me and Stefan are going to take very good care of you, and soon when the Germans have gone you'll be with your family again." It was a challenge for Marta to hold back the tears herself when tears begin to run down Sara's cheeks, and yet the girl didn't make a sound, bravely trying to hold in her feelings. Even when Matous said goodbye, she didn't break down but Marta knew Sara's heart must be breaking.

Marta sought to distract her. "We're going to have a lot of fun together you and I. Do you like puppets?" Sara nodded. Marta could tell the nod was given out of good manners rather than enthusiasm. "I thought you might. We'll go down to Stefan's workshop when you've finished your drink. I'm sure he'll let you pick one to keep as your very own."

Matous didn't break down until he got home.

Only days later the family were forced to move to Josefov. Their new home was but one room. The ghetto was overflowing with new arrivals evicted from their accommodation elsewhere in the city. They had become a human zoo, caged in a small area of the city, but a zoo ignored by the rest of the population. Matous spent time in the small Jewish cemetery when he wanted some alone time. Hundreds of grave stones leaned at precarious angles impossibly close together. Many had blackened with time and their inscriptions had become indistinct. He wondered what would happen to his family and whether they would even be remembered with a grave stone.

Each day the Rubinsteins waited, waited for their turn to come. Many other families had already departed. It wasn't many weeks until Matous received their transport notices.

On a foggy February morning, they stood with their luggage at the nearest tram stop in the half light. Passers by emerged out of the opaqueness to be swallowed by the gloom seconds later as if they had been but phantoms. Matous was seized with the thought of taking his family and doing the same, disappearing. But when the fog lifted tomorrow, if not today, they would be caught and punished. Not for them the freedom to walk down a street and live in a home.

He heard the tram before he could see it, but they couldn't get on the first one because it consisted of only one carriage. Jews were only permitted

to travel standing at the back in the second carriage. It was more than half an hour until a two
carriage tram arrived by which time the bleak
dampness had penetrated their very souls, com-
pounding the melancholy they already felt. The
tram rattled noisily along and crossed the Vltava
to the Trade Fair Palace. There were no trade
fairs held there any more and 'palace' seemed a
wholly inappropriate name for the stark, mod-
ernist building that it was.

The family were required to wait in a long line
and hand over any money and jewellery they had
brought with them. Matous had already completed an inventory of all they possessed before
leaving their apartment to move to the ghetto.
He had brought his violin and was relieved the
unfeeling eyes of the human magpies snatching
people's heirlooms and sentimental possessions
were uninterested in his instrument or his son's.
Music might be the only solace where they were
going.

The men of the family were then ordered to join
another queue. Afterwards, they rejoined Raisa
and her mother-in-law. Matous had expected the
two women to be shocked at the sight of their
shaven heads but they had already observed the
other men around them.

"I've always thought bald men were handsome,"
said Raisa in an effort to cheer up her son whose
expression was particularly glum. He had had
such an attractive shock of dark brown hair.

"How can they do that to you all? It makes you look like convicts, it's so dehumanising," said her mother-in-law unhelpfully.

White lines in two metre squares had been painted on the floor of the cavernous exhibition space. Each family was assigned one. Matous and Jakub went to get a couple of mattresses from a large pile by one wall. They were stained and smelled unpleasant. Despite the cold inside the unheated building, Matous' mother insisted that her husband first take off his coat and lay it down on the space where she wished to sit. Sit was all they could do. There wasn't enough room for them all to lie down, and no one was supposed to leave their assigned area unless commanded to do so. It made the one room which they had lived in during their time in Josefov seem positively large.

After a miserable couple of days, they along with hundreds of others were herded like cattle through the streets of Prague to the station. Some of the Czechs they passed gave looks of sympathy but several either ignored them or looked at them as if they were the source of a nasty smell.

"I'm glad Sarinka isn't here with us, it was so uncomfortable back there," said Raisa to her husband.

Matous merely nodded, he knew this was only the beginning of something worse but he didn't share that thought with Raisa.

CHAPTER 25

Sara stood at the window watching snow perform its ethereal dance while it fell gently towards the ground. The sound of children's unrestrained joy in the street below as they threw snowballs rose towards the apartment. Noticing Sara's dejected look at not being able to join them, Marta placed her hand on Sara's shoulder.

"One day you'll be out there again, and we're all going to have the biggest party ever. We'll dance in the streets, and you shall have whatever you want."

Sara raised her head towards Marta. "Will I ever see my parents again? And Jakub?"

Marta wanted to say yes, of course she would, but something in Sara's disarmingly frank expression told her that Sara wanted honesty more than anything else.

"I hope and pray so, Sarinka. There's something I need to show you." Marta went over to one of the two armchairs and pushed it out of the way and then pulled back the rug on which it had stood. "Just in case the Germans were to come here searching, we've made a safe space for you." Getting down on her knees, Marta lifted a couple of floorboards and put them to one side. "It's rather cramped I know but I've put a couple of blankets and a pillow down there to make it more comfortable. Did you want to try it? It might be an idea to get used to it so that it won't seem strange if you ever have to use it."

Sara didn't reply and slid herself with obvious reluctance into the confined space as if a dog only doing so because it was what her owner wanted of her. It was as horrible as a medieval oubliette. Marta put the floor boards back in place.

Considering that it was little different to burying the child alive, Marta removed them after just a few seconds. Sara looked as traumatised by the experience as Marta had feared she would be. How she felt for Sara, so much of her childhood stolen. How she must wish to run and play, to feel snowflakes caress her face and the crisp, cold air in the back of her throat. Would the girl grow to be an adult imprisoned in this apartment? If Germany won the war, she might never be able to set foot outside again.

Marta did what she was qualified to do and devoted herself to Sara's education. It was one thing Marta could control in these awful times when so much that she wanted for herself and others she was powerless to make happen. If freedom should come she wanted Sara to have the best chance possible to make something of her life.

With only ration coupons for two, Marta and Stefan went to bed hungry every night. They kept their portions small to ensure Sara never did. When Stefan complained of always being hungry as they lay in bed, Marta retorted:

"It's good for us, we could both do with losing a few kilos." That wasn't true, they were already thin.

She also wanted another sacrifice. "I think it's time to stop the gun running, Stefan. We have Sara to think about now. If you were caught, this apartment would be ransacked and they'd find her. How could we ever face Matous and Raisa again if we let that happen."

"I'm not sure we will ever see them again," answered her husband. "I need to do my part. We'll never get rid of the Germans if we don't take risks."

"You've already played your part. It's time for someone else to do it, for Sara's sake."

"All right, I'll think about it."

Matous and his family were sixty kilometres outside of Prague in Terezin, or Theriesenstadt, a former garrison town for the Austro-Hungarian Empire. In the dilapidated and unsanitary barracks, thousands were obliged to live in spaces meant only for hundreds. On arrival, the men and boys were separated from the women and girls.

Matous' mother and father tearfully embraced,

and Jakub hugged his mother tightly. Matous and Raisa gave each other half smiles, their love had withered too long ago for a display of affection. On their walk from the Trade Fair Palace to the station, Raisa had seen her once again, wrapped in a fur coat and watching the sorry procession. The pained expression in the woman's eyes had been mirrored by Matous when he too spotted her. They might no longer be able to indulge their passion for each other but Raisa could see the love in his eyes for Radmila.

Matous was thankful that Sara wasn't here with them when he saw the dormitory in which they were to live. Crude wooden bunk beds three stories high with over sixty in each room. He, his father and Jakub had to share just one single bed with only a thin blanket between them.

Although not an extermination camp, conditions were harsh and disease rampant, and over thirty thousand would die here.

Observing Matous' look of horror at the room, a man commented:

"Don't look so miserable. Just pray they don't put you on one of the transports to the East. It is said those who go there will never return."

Through the window which had not been cleaned in years, Jakub looked down on a blurred courtyard below. He could discern nine men who appeared to be of a similar age to him carrying shovels as guards drove them forward with

DAVID CANFORD

the encouragement of their rifle butts. "What's going on?"

"They wrote to their mothers without permission," said the man. "They're being taken off to dig their own graves." Almost as horrific as what Jakub was witnessing, was the man's matter of fact tone as if what the Nazis did no longer had the power to shock him or instil outrage.

That first night, the three male Rubinsteins got little sleep. Even though they were exhausted, each time one of them turned over, they woke up the others. The next evening, Matous volunteered to lie on the floor to give the other two a chance to sleep.

The food they received was barely enough to keep Matous and Jakub going. Elderly and thus exempt from work, Matous' father was given even less. He refused attempts by Matous to share his meagre rations.

"I'm old and resigned to my fate. But you need to stay strong, my son, and Jakub too so that you can both survive."

Matous and Jakub were assigned to do carpentry and counted themselves fortunate. Some were sent to work in the coal mines in nearby Kladno, spending not only their nights in blackness but their days also. Matous' question as to what Raisa was doing was answered one morning when he saw her walking across the courtyard and into the laundry.

Matous knew he, Raisa and Jakub had a good

165

chance of surviving Terezin if only they could remain here. Each time the guards announced the numbers of those who were to leave and go 'East', Matous would listen on tenterhooks as if waiting for a trap door to open underneath him. The stress was almost more than he could bare.

At last, spring chased away winter. In Prague, Marta tossed and turned in her bed. Sleep didn't come easy these days. She worried about Sara. The girl spoke so infrequently. She had withdrawn into herself like a clam in a shell. And Marta wondered about Klara. Marta had never returned to where her daughter lived since that Christmas when she had left a present on the doorstep. And of course there was also Pavel to worry about. Marta couldn't understand how Stefan could possibly be snoring within minutes of his head hitting the pillow.

Marta decided to get up. In the living area, she switched on the light, took a book from her shelf and settled down in the armchair. Reading was an escape. While absorbed in a novel she wasn't fretting about her family. Her imagination flew out of the window to the world described in the book, a world where Nazis didn't exist.

The turning of the front door handle abruptly dropped her back in reality and made the hairs on the back of her neck stand on end. She jumped up, clutching her book against her chest as though it might protect her from the intruder. At one time they had never needed to lock the door, nobody had, but things were different now. She had no idea who it could possibly be at this time of night other than someone of bad intent. The knock which followed was soft as if the person didn't want others to know he or she was in the building, hardly the approach the police would have taken, she concluded.

"Who is it?" called out Marta uncertainly.

"It's me."

CHAPTER 26

Marta immediately recognised the voice and turned the key in the lock, her heart swelling with emotion.

"Paja," she uttered in delight as she opened the door and flung her arms around her son. "Thank God you're alive. Let me look at you." She stood back and smiled to see that he appeared well fed and healthy. "I must go wake your father."

Stefan appeared in his pyjamas and embraced the young man.

"Will you wake Klara?" asked Pavel.

"She doesn't live here anymore, she got married," replied Marta.

"Married? I wish I had more time so I could hear all the news but I can't stay. I'm here on a mission. I can't tell you what it is. I just wanted to let you know that I'm all right. I didn't want to write from England for fear of compromising you."

Marta's brief moment of joy was swept aside by a flood of anxiety. "Why couldn't you have stayed in England and fought from there?"

"Because there's nothing I can do in England. Hitler has mainland Europe under his control.

Maybe now the Russians and Americans are in the war, the Allies will invade but that could take years. I was offered the chance to do something for my country so I took it. Try not to worry, I'll be careful. I love you both." He hugged them again. "I should go now in case anyone notices me. Before I go I wanted to give you this." Pavel reached inside his pocket while he spoke and handed them a small photograph. "I met a wonderful woman in England. Susan is my wife's name, and we have a baby son, six months old. We named him Stanislav, and when this war ends they'll both come here to live."

His parents watched him leave. Neither could sleep, the relief of knowing that their son was alive had been crushed by knowing that he had returned to the lion's den. To do what they didn't know, but whatever it was must be extremely dangerous and carry a high risk of death.

Marta kissed the black and white photo Pavel had left. The woman had wavy hair and a pleasant smile, and Marta's grandson a little tuft of hair on his head and chubby arms and legs and eyes which were laughing.

In the days which followed Marta dreaded there being another knock on the door, someone come to give her terrible news. She had rarely listened to the radio since the invasion but now she took to switching in on regularly. Stress seized her each time the news was broadcast, making her feel sick with worry. She fully expected to hear a report of a failed attack and a righteous gloating that the perpetrators had been shot. The torment of waiting was there day after day, an unwelcome guest who refused to leave.

Three weeks after their son's visit, Stefan was pushing his puppet theatre through the north east of the city, returning from making a delivery of weapons. He had ignored Marta's plea to stop. His son's sacrifices made him determined to continue. A man rushed past him, bumping into Stefan as he did so and nearly knocking him over. "Hey!" protested Stefan. He turned to admonish the man but the man ignored him, his focus was elsewhere. From under his raincoat he had produced a machine gun and was aiming at a man being driven past in an open top green Mercedes. Transfixed, Stefan watched events unfold. The man's gun jammed and the passenger, a German officer, yelled at his driver to stop and drew his pistol to fire at the would be assassin. Stefan recognised the German from the newspapers. With his aquiline nose and small, mean eyes, he was the most senior Nazi in the country and the most hated, Reinhard Heydrich.

Another man threw a grenade which exploded by the rear of the car sending fragments flying. The windows of a tram opposite shattered and screams came from within. Stefan's attention was grabbed by a couple of SS jackets which had been hurled upwards by the blast from the car seats where they had lain, landing on the overhead tram wires like demonic scarecrows.

Heydrich, clearly wounded, got out of his car. Together with his driver, he advanced towards the attackers. The man who had thrown the grenade jumped on his bicycle and pedalled away firing his pistol into the air to disperse passengers emerging from the tram who were blocking his escape route.

Stefan took shelter behind his mobile theatre and hearing further shots peeped out to determine where they were coming from. The man with the machine gun which had jammed was crouched by a telegraph pole firing a pistol at Heydrich who was returning fire. Suddenly, Heydrich collapsed in pain and the man ran off and into a nearby butcher's shop. The owner ran out pointing and shouting. Heydrich's driver raced up to the doorway. The noise of further gunfire erupted. The would be assassin came out of the shop and ran off, jumping aboard a passing tram.

Stefan didn't wait to see if Heydrich was dead. Gut wrenching anxiety was strangling him. He needed to get out of here. And what about Pavel? Where was he? Had he been involved in planning the attack? Was that the mission, to kill Hitler's number three? If they had succeeded, Stefan would shed no tears for that monster Heydrich but the reprisals would be severe. And if Pavel was caught, he would face indescribable torture before they murdered him.

All the way back home Stefan expected to hear a shout to stop. He didn't know if he would keep going or obey should that happen. Would they be less likely to search his home and arrest Marta also if he ignored their order and they shot him dead?

Reaching his building, Stefan bumped his theatre down the stairs to his workshop, almost losing his balance as he did so. Once inside, he noticed several bullet holes. He needed to destroy his theatre and get rid of the weapons and ammunition hidden in the workshop in case Pavel was captured and the Nazis raided their home.

Even if his son wasn't caught, he knew he must get rid of the theatre. The SS would already be interrogating those passengers from the tram. One might well mention a man with a puppet theatre. No longer could he risk being seen pushing it around Prague. Frantically he began pulling the theatre apart. Tears streamed down his face as he did so, not because the theatre had been such a large part of his life for so long, but because he couldn't stop thinking of something much worse. His son might never get to see his own son grow up.

Marta was sitting at the table dabbing her eyes with a handkerchief when Stefan went up to the apartment.

"Heydrich's been attacked, he's in hospital. It was on the radio. You know what that means."

Stefan sat down next to her and laid his hand

on hers. "It's all right, I was passing by as it happened. Pavel wasn't there."

"But he must be involved somehow. Why else would he have come back to Prague? What if they catch him?"

"We must pray they don't."

Stefan waited until after midnight to carry the remains of his theatre upstairs. If a neighbour saw him, they might ask what he was doing and report him to the authorities. Although they opened the window, Stefan and Marta had droplets of sweat dripping from their foreheads as they burned the wood on the fire that late May night. Stefan didn't tell Marta that he still had guns and ammunition to get rid of. He had always thought he could throw them into the Vltava or arrange for a contact to come pick them up if he needed to but that would have to wait. The streets would be crawling with police and soldiers intent on finding Heydrich's attackers.

Marta too had a secret which she hadn't shared with Stefan. She had a new pupil up at the castle where Heydrich had installed himself when he had taken over from his predecessor. The son of Heydrich's number two, Karl Hermann Frank.

CHAPTER 27

The day Marta had walked up to the castle to meet Frank at the beginning of April, she had wanted to leave almost as soon as she had been allowed through the tall iron gates. She hadn't gone voluntarily. The father of one of her students was a German officer who worked in the castle.

"I mentioned how much our daughter has improved since you began giving her lessons to Gruppenführer Frank," said the man when she arrived one afternoon at his house to teach his child. "He expects to see you in his office at ten tomorrow morning. His son is struggling with his studies and needs help."

The man didn't make it sound that turning down the unwelcome invitation was an option. Marta decided not to mention the matter to Stefan just as she had never mentioned that she gave private tuition to any Germans. He would have objected and demanded that she stop, yet Marta couldn't see the harm in it. After all, why shouldn't she relieve them of some of their money. They were happy to pay the rates she charged, which were considerably higher than those she asked Czech families to pay. With the enhanced rates she received from Germans, Marta taught the children of poorer Czech customers for free. But helping Frank's son was something she would definitely have preferred to avoid.

Before the invasion, Frank had been a leading light in the Sudeten German Party which had lobbied Hitler to take over the Sudetenland, and he had since become a committed member of the Nazi party. He had worked eagerly with Heydrich in ramping up arrests and executions and accelerating the number of Jews sent off to concentration camps.

Inside, a soldier asked her to follow and marched at speed down the long, sombre corridor, forcing Marta to almost run to keep up. He clicked his heels together and stood to one side to let her enter through huge double doors into a large room overlooking Saint Vitus Cathedral, the holy centre of Czech identity, now surrounded by the immorality of Nazism.

The man sitting at the desk in the far corner of the room looked up and beckoned her to approach with a flick of his index finger as if summoning a servant. He had a high forehead and thick eyebrows. His black hair was swept backwards and his countenance was severe. He appeared to be in his mid forties, the same age as Stefan.

"Frau Janicek, I have heard very good reports of

your teaching abilities. I want you to help my son. You will come here Tuesdays and Thursdays at four for one hour. My son will be waiting in the adjacent room. Understood?"

Marta gave a brief nod, the man intimidated her. She forced herself to speak, hoping her inner nervousness wasn't apparent. "Are there any particular areas you would like me to address?"

"That will be for you to decide when you have assessed him. You may go now." He gave a dismissive wave of his hand to indicate the meeting was over, though she considered that much preferable to a "Heil Hitler" which she would have felt compelled to replicate even though the Nazi salute was so abhorrent to her..

The boy had an angelic face despite his father's looks, which Marta concluded meant the boy must have inherited his features from his mother. Yet his Hitler Youth uniform contradicted the idea that he would be likeable. He was only twelve but already arrogant.

"I don't understand why my father has hired you, a Czech," he complained the first time they met after his father had returned to his office after introducing her.

Marta knew how to handle him. "Because your father wants the best. Now do you want me to report to him that you are unhappy with his choice?" He lowered his head sheepishly and shook it. "All right, let's begin."

Marta may have got the upper hand, but she

didn't enjoy her time there, at the centre of hate and oppression. She always breathed a sigh of relief when she left the castle and descended the hill on her way home, gulping in the view of Prague spread before her like an antidote. From this vantage point, she could forget for one moment the way things were and imagine that the Nazis had never taken over her city, suffocating all that had been wonderful about it.

Visiting the castle twice a week and teaching the son of a murderer became harder after Pavel had visited her. And worse still when Heydrich was attacked. When the man died a week later, the Germans' rage, directed by Frank himself, intensified. Receiving intelligence that one of those involved in the assassination came from Lidice, a village not far from the capital, the Nazis massacred all the men in the village, sent the women off to concentration camps and took the children away for 're-education'. It later transpired that they were gassed.

On the radio it was announced that if by 18 June no one had come forward with information leading to the capture of the assassins further reprisals would follow. Stefan returned home pale. "There's word on the street that they've found the partisans hiding in the Cathedral of Saint Cyril and Methodius and a battle is raging."

Marta put her hand to her mouth to stifle a cry. Sara who was sitting at the table drawing, got up and went into her room. That evening the radio confirmed the news. Seven traitors had been 'liquidated' but no names were given. Once again Stefan and Marta were in that dark cave of torment, not knowing if their son was still alive, desperately hoping. This time hope seemed a delusion.

The following day, Marta went to the castle with one purpose. She wanted to know one way or the other. Maybe she would overhear something, but despite the self-congratulatory voices that the perpetrators were dead no names were mentioned within her hearing.

She paced up and down while her pupil sat attempting the algebra she had set him, frustrated she could do nothing to get an answer to her question.

"I'll be back in an hour," boomed a voice from the corridor. Marta stopped in her tracks, it was the voice of Frank. She looked at the dark brown door separating the room she was in from his desk.

"There's someone I need to talk to, I'll only be gone a few minutes." The boy responded with a grunt. Opening the door to the corridor, she looked along it. It was deserted. She turned right and went a few metres. Her clammy hands slipping against the doorknob to Frank's room, she entered it. Her mouth was dry as dust, her pulse racing. Marta was alone in the office of the country's most senior Nazi, something which would surely have her executed were she to be caught.

She started leafing through a pile the papers on Frank's desk, quickly scanning them as she sought an answer. She found nothing but there were more.

"What are you doing in here?" The words made Marta jump and she moved back from the desk. The boy stood at the interconnecting door, his look one of triumph.

"I… your father said he had a letter for me. I was just seeing if I could locate it as he wasn't here." The explanation sounded feeble. She needed to reassert her authority. "I'll have to ask him later. And why have you left your desk? Did you finish your assignment?" The boy suddenly looked less sure of himself. "No, I thought you hadn't, now get back to it." Marta followed him into the side room. Standing behind him, she wrung her hands, desperate for the lesson to end before Frank's return.

Marta walked home as quickly as she could without drawing attention to herself and barged into the workshop.

"We're in danger. Sara's in danger."

"What do you mean?" said Stefan getting up from his stool.

"I've been giving lessons up at the castle to Frank's son."

"Frank's son! Why on earth-"

"This is no time for a lecture. While the boy was working I went into Frank's office and went through his papers to see if I could see Paja's name, to see if he was one of those killed at the cathedral. While I was doing so his son saw me. I feel sure he'll tell his father. We need to move Sara."

"Where to?"

"Klara's."

"But she's married to a German."

"There's no one else we can turn to. If they come for us, they'll surely rip the place apart, and even if they don't find Sara, how is she going to survive alone if they arrest us?"

CHAPTER 28

"Sarinka, I need you to be very brave." Marta knelt before the bewildered child, holding both her hands in hers. "We need to move you. It's not safe for you here any longer. I'm taking you somewhere else."

Sara's face crumpled. "I don't want to go, I like it here."

"I know. We don't want you to go either, but we don't have a choice. Trust me."

"But what if we're stopped? I have no papers."

"We won't be. A woman and a girl together, why it's the most natural thing of all. Now let's pack your things into my shopping bag."

When they walked towards the tram stop, Sara gripped Marta's hand tightly as if she would be ripped away from her should she let go. Riding on the tram felt a little safer, but each time she saw a soldier or policeman on a street corner, Sara lowered her head, scared of being noticed.

It was only a short walk to Klara's apartment. Marta prayed that her daughter would be at home.

"Mamka?" Klara looked stunned as she opened

the door.

"Can we come in?" Marta didn't wait for an answer before entering.

"What brings you here and with…"

"Sara, Matous and Raisa's daughter. I need your help. Your father and I have been looking after her but she's not safe at ours any longer. I want you to take care of her."

Klara's mouth dropped open. "But-" A baby's cry interrupted her.

Marta gave her that look which mothers give their daughters.

"That's Greta. I'll go get her." Returning with the baby, Klara placed her in Marta's arms.

"Oh, my little sweetheart." Marta beamed at her. Greta gave her grandmother a toothless grin. It was such a bitter sweet moment, one of intense joy but also of devastating sadness.

"I don't know what Jürgen will say about what you're asking."

"You're a mother now, Klara. Imagine if Greta were Sara. Make me proud of you, darling. I must go. I love you, never forget that." She handed Greta back to her daughter and walked out of the apartment before she wept. She didn't want them to see that. Her legs were lead as she made her way back and her heart bleeding with sorrow.

They came almost the moment that she got home, the heavy footfalls on the stairs the ominous precursor of the inevitable.

Though she screamed out in pain when she was tortured after her arrest, Marta's greatest pain was the realisation that she was most probably never going to see her granddaughter again and would never get to meet her grandson and would never know if Sara was safe. She had only one comfort. The angry interrogator, whose breath smelled of excrement and whose manic shouting, his face only centimetres away, covered hers in sprays of spit, didn't once ask her about Pavel. Surely that meant they couldn't have found him among the bodies. The torture was relentless because there was nothing Marta could confess to. She would never reveal that she had been seeking information about her son.

Stefan endured a similar experience. When he asked about Marta, they promised to tell him if he confessed so he didn't find out. Eventually, they gave up and let him go, pushing him from their vehicle outside his building like a bag of foul smelling garbage. His body black and blue and with several broken ribs, each step up to the apartment hurt. But opening the door to the apartment was a bigger hurt. His calls for Marta were unanswered, instead a loud silence enveloped him. Things remained exactly as they had been the day when they had come for them. Drawers open, their contents strewn across the floor, broken plates, scattered clothing, and the mattress slit open as if it had suffered a frenzied knife attack. Stefan hauled himself to the bed and surrendered to sleep.

In the days and weeks which followed, he waited. Waited for Marta to fill the empty void and bring life back to his world. Stefan regretted that he had failed to tell Marta he loved her and ask for her forgiveness, and now it was likely too late. He had been unworthy of her and yet it was she who had surely died, not him.

Stefan survived on memories, memories of when this tired old apartment had echoed to love and laughter and the precious gift of a family. The present seemed too unkind a place to dwell. He didn't know if he had any family left other than a grandson whose mother he had no way of contacting and a daughter who had joined the enemy.

Stefan was unaware that he had a granddaughter. Taken away separately, Marta didn't get a chance to tell him, tell him something that might have melted the ice in his heart where Klara was concerned.

Sometimes Stefan wished they had killed him. Maybe they would have if he hadn't taken the two rifles and ammunition from his workshop and abandoned them in an alleyway when Marta had taken Sara to Klara's.

In Terezin, life and death were close companions. Matous spent his nights wedged between his father and Jakub. The morning that Matous felt no warmth coming from his father's body he knew instantly. Old age or perhaps despair had claimed him.

Matous worried about Jakub dying. He was only in the spring of life. Poor sanitation and over-crowding allowed disease to rampage. It had no preference for the old. When they were confined to their block because of an outbreak of typhus at the camp, Matous hated the feeling of helpless-ness. It had been close to a miracle that Rudi had recovered all those years ago in Russia. He didn't know if Jakub would be so lucky. When two in their dormitory went down with it, Matous felt sick in the pit of his stomach as the ropes of anx-iety tightened around him. Was it wrong to ask God that if he must take a member of his fam-ily to choose Raisa or Yosef instead? That is what he did. He didn't love the other two like he did Jakub, and he needed to stay alive himself to help protect his son however he could. Whether or not Matous' plea worked, Jakub didn't succumb to the disease and neither did Matous.

The Nazis allowed a cultural life to exist. Matous and Jakub were left free to join others to play their violins in the dank basement of the bar-racks. It was their only escape from their miser-able existence. As he played, Matous closed his eyes and imagined he was back in the great con-cert halls of Europe with their ceiling decoration, elaborate balconies and enormous chandeliers. He could almost sense the euphoria of those standing ovations and the cheers, no one caring about nationality or religion, all united in the uplifting joy of music. At night, his mind flew back to Paris. Once again he strolled arm in arm with Radmila along the city's elegant boulevards late in the evening after a concert, and recalled their intimate dinners in a bistro and the ecstasy of her love in their small hotel room overlooking the Notre Dame.

Matous was introduced to the Czech composer Rafael Schaechter, also imprisoned in Terezin. He had established a choir of both men and women and was preparing them for a performance of Smetana's 'The Bartered Bride', the first Czech opera to achieve international acclaim.

"I'd like you and your son to play first and second violin," said the man.

"We are the only violins."

"Exactly." That made Matous laugh, the first time he had done so since arriving.

Schaechter had only one score and everyone had to learn their pieces by heart,. Raisa was a member of the choir. Jakub was thrilled to spend time again with his mother. The weariness that weighed her down like a stone slab tied to her back, and which made her seem so much older than her forty years, disappeared as her face shone at being with her son again.

"How's grandma?" he asked after they had embraced.

"Cantankerous as ever but we manage. I thought

maybe grandpa's passing would have finished her, but she's a tough old bird. I think she's even grown to like me after all these years, the Russian peasant who stole her only son."

"Well it only took two decades," said Matous who had come to join them.

Schaechter tapped his baton loudly. "Time to rehearse everybody."

After weeks of practice, the end result was far from perfection. It was so much more than that, it was a victory for the irrepressible human spirit, and for dignity in the face of so much inhumanity. Life affirming voices which refused to be beaten.

After the performance given to other inmates when Jakub went over to talk to his grandmother, Raisa approached Matous. Her expression was disturbingly serious in the light of the rapturous reaction which the audience had given them.

"Your mother and I have been told that we're to be transported tomorrow." The colour drained from Matous' face. "I don't want you to tell Jakub, he'll want to come too. So often when a family member receives their order to go East, the rest of the family volunteers to go with them, and I know Jakub would."

"But I can't lie to him, tell him that I didn't know. He'll hate me forever."

"Then tell him if you must but please don't let him come, I'm begging you. I couldn't bear what I will have to if I knew that he was there suffering as well. If I die, I want to believe that he has lived, that all my children have." Raisa maintained her composure even though every fibre of her being must have been trying to make her release a flood of emotion.

"I'm so sorry, Raisa. Sorry that I uprooted you from Russia. You would have been so much safer in Irkutsk."

"Maybe, but safety's not what counts in life. I would never have had Jakub and Sara if I had stayed. They, together with Yosef, are the greatest gifts I have received. We loved each other once, Matous, and our children came from love. Goodbye, and take good care of yourself. Our children need you." Raisa went to join Jakub and her mother, putting on the painted smile of a clown.

"I'm going with her," insisted Jakub that evening when Matous told his son as they sat on the hard wood of their bunk.

"But it's not what she wants, you have to respect her wishes."

"I want to be there to protect her."

"I know you do, Jakub. But you can't, neither of us can. If you go, you'll be separated from her, just like here. Don't add to her heartache, please."

Jakub exhaled with anger and frustration. "I'm sleeping in the corridor."

Not that he nor his father slept that night. As day was breaking, Matous went out into the corridor to find his son but he had gone. Matous raced along it and down the stairs, catching up with Jakub by the door.

"Get off me!" Jakub yelled as his father touched his shoulder. Jakub stormed out into a grey, crepuscular light. Matous followed at a distance. Jakub went out of the courtyard and through another to where a line of figures, heads bowed, shuffled slowly forward as guards prodded them with the end of their rifles to keep them moving. Jakub stopped and shouted, his words loud and clear. "I love you."

Matous saw a head turn briefly. He couldn't discern features in this light but he was certain it was her. On she went and out of the gates, arm in arm with the old woman by her side.

Matous went over to his son, holding him as he lay his head on his father's shoulder and wept.

CHAPTER 29

"Come on or we'll be late for the performance." Violin in hand, Matous had already got down from their bunk.

"What's the point?" complained his son. Since his mother's departure some months earlier, Jakub had retreated into a carapace of gloom and apathy. In what should have been the best years of his life, he was incarcerated and awaiting a worse punishment for having committed no crime.

"Because it's probably keeping us from being transported, that's why," said his father.

"So we can go on being the Nazi's puppets, you mean."

"The longer we can be, the better the chance we'll still be here to be freed when the war ends."

"If it ever does, and who's to say Hitler won't win it." With a sour expression, Jakub slid down.

Terezin had only recently received a makeover. Buildings had been painted, a school created although it had no pupils, flowers planted, and even a coffee house established. A large number of those trapped in Terezin were hurriedly shipped off to Auschwitz to avoid conveying an appearance of overcrowding. 'Operation Embellishment' was aimed to deflect rumours of inhumane treatment and extermination camps when the International Red Cross were permitted to visit in June 1944. The highlight of their inspection was to be a rendition of Verdi's Requiem. Musicians and a choir of over one hundred were to perform. It was something they had done before for pleasure but were now compelled to do, the victims forced to play their part in upholding a terrible lie.

High ranking Nazis and Red Cross officials sat in the first row like admiring parents at a school play. Jakub wanted to shout out that it was all a cruel deception and the Red Cross were being fooled. He failed to do so, instead clinging like others to the hope that somehow if he only did as he was told he would survive.

More humiliation was to come. In September, they had to repeat it all again for a Nazi propaganda film shot by one of the prisoners, Kurt Gerron, who had been a film director and actor. It was too late to shout out now. Any dissension would be left on the cutting room floor.

"I knew we shouldn't have been their puppets," said Jakub not long afterwards while he and his father queued for some watery soup and stale bread at the end of a day's work. "We should have told the truth when we had the chance."

"We're still here, aren't we?"

"You haven't heard, have you."

"Heard what?"

"Both Schaechter and Gerron have been sent East. If what they did couldn't save them, then nothing we can do will save us. Can't you see that?"

Matous' shoulders fell, his plan to avoid being sent to the death camps was mocking him. It was inevitable, only a matter of when.

On Valentine's day 1945 in his workshop in Prague, Stefan stopped carving and lifted his head sharply when he heard loud thuds. He hurried outside to investigate. Like vultures high above the city, some fifty bombers were flying westwards. Others too had come out onto the street.

"Do you know what's happening?" Stefan asked the man next to him..

"It must be the Allies but I don't know why they attacked us."

The planes dropped no more bombs. Stefan joined a crowd heading towards the river. On the opposite bank, black smoke billowed upwards from the direction of Charles Square and Vysehrad, the old castle district.

"Damn the Allies, they're no better than the Nazis. First they abandon us, and now they come to kill us," complained an angry old woman in a black headscarf.

"Maybe it was a mistake," said a young man near

her. "Perhaps they thought they were over Germany. At least it must mean the Allies are making progress."

It was indeed a mistake. The American bombers had thought they were over Dresden and there were no more Allied air raids on Prague.

Life in the city was becoming ever more difficult and most were going hungry. Many shops were empty with nothing left to sell. Instead, they displayed the poster required by the authorities, 'Closed for victory of the Reich'. Garbage went uncollected and the streets reeked of decay. The trams were dirty and broke down often. Working hours for Czechs had been extended to increase arms production, and even Sunday was now a working day. The inhabitants longed for the war to be over quickly. If not, their survival would become ever more precarious.

At the end of April, rumours spread that American troops were in the west of the country and advancing towards Prague. News also filtered through that Berlin had fallen and Hitler was dead. In the streets was a tangible sense that the end was near. All it required was for someone to light the fuse. That came with an impassioned call from Czechoslovak radio, which had stopped broadcasting what the Nazis wanted. The radio announcer described how the radio station was under attack and asked citizens to come and help defend it. Then came a plea to set up barricades all over the city.

As hated swastikas were torn down and Czech flags were hung from windows once more, Stefan joined others in his district. In heavy rain which made the grey pavements almost shine, they pushed a tram onto its side to block the main road into Mala Strana. Not many German troops remained in the city, but word had reached the defenders that there were thousands assembling on the outskirts. Few Czechs were armed and so they tore up cobbles to hurl although they understood their defiance would have little impact against the weapons they would face. Soon those resisting farther out had retreated to the centre in the face of overwhelming odds.

"I don't understand why the Americans aren't helping," said Stefan to the man by his side as they waited for the Nazi forces to appear.

"They say they've agreed that the Russians are to take the city."

"And where the hell are they when we need them?"

"Who knows."

Stefan wondered if today was the day he would die. If so, so be it, he told himself. Yet the enemy didn't appear and come dusk he went back home. The following day, Stefan crossed Charles Bridge to find out what he could. As he reached the Old Town Square his spirits sank. Bodies lay face down as though felled by a virulent plague. Flames erupted from what had once been the

windows of The Old Town Hall and other buildings while German tanks stood swivelling their
turrets like enraged beasts intent on revenge.
His beautiful city was going to be razed to the
ground, destroyed when the war was so nearly
finished.

Suddenly, cheering ran down the side streets,
a river of joy bursting the dam of occupation.
Voices excitedly passed on the message. "Germany's surrendered, the war is over."

It wasn't long before German tank crews began
to emerge, hands above their heads. Stefan felt
his own hand grabbed by a woman he didn't
know. She pulled him towards a circle of people
dancing with happiness. His head spun. After six
long years, the darkness was ending and Czechoslovakia would finally be free again.

The day after, crowds lined the streets and threw
flowers at Soviet tanks and troops as they entered the city. Little did they know that their 'lib-
erators' had their own agenda for the future of
the country.

Sitting atop one tank, smiling broadly and admiring the city which he hadn't seen for so long
was a twenty-seven year old man. Yosef Rubinstein had felt as though he never quite belonged
in his own family, as if he were somehow different to his siblings. In the Soviet Union, he had
found a system which appealed to his sense of re-
jection and had given him a purpose in life.

CHAPTER 30

Stefan didn't go out onto the streets to greet the Soviets. The war was over but the life he once had no longer existed, and peace wouldn't bring it back. The dagger of loss was sharper now. Watching people celebrating only served to accentuate his loneliness.

He tried to comfort himself by thinking of how there need be no more hiding. No longer need he fear that his neighbours might report him, that a word out of place could have him arrested. He could say out loud what he believed. He would be able to vote again. He could wear his Legionnaire's medal and speak proudly of how he fought the Soviets, a feat which had generated the international support for the creation of his country. Yet freedom without family to share it with didn't make him feel any better.

Stefan's closest companions had bright eyes and big smiles but they only opened their mouths if he pulled their strings, and any words they spoke came from him. Still, he didn't have to talk to them if he didn't want to, which suited him as most of the time he didn't feel like talking to anyone, not even himself. A vortex of melancholy was pulling him ever deeper into a solitary world where he disliked daylight and welcomed the night.

He was irritated when eating a bowl of cabbage soup for his dinner, he had to get up to answer a knock on the door. He didn't want visitors who would ask how he was and probably tell him that he needed to get out more.

"Father!" Pavel wrapped Stefan in a bear hug.

"My boy, I can't believe it, I was convinced you had perished."

"Where's mother?" asked Pavel when his father finally let go of him.

"I'm afraid she's dead, son."

"How?"

Pavel sat down and put his elbows on the table and his head in his hands as his father explained. When Pavel removed his hands, his eyes were red. Stefan felt for him, his son's return mirrored his own from Russia, a mother lost, leaving a hole that couldn't be filled.

"She would have been so happy to know that you're alive. You were her pride and joy."

That was too much, Pavel couldn't contain his feelings and wept.

"Have you thought what you'll do now the war's ended?" asked Stefan once Pavel had calmed.

"Go fetch my wife and son and bring them back to Prague."

"How wonderful, I can't wait to meet them. You

can all live here."

"Thank you. I'll find our own place as soon as I can. How's Klara?"

"I don't know. She married a German, I haven't seen her in years."

"A German?" asked Pavel, shocked at the news.

"A German Czech, but that makes no difference. They all sided with the Nazis, and he worked for the Protectorate Police. We were hiding Matous and Raisa's daughter, Sara, here. When we knew the Nazis were coming for us, your mother took Sara to Klara's. It seemed a crazy thing to do to me."

"What happened to her?"

"I don't know."

"You mean you haven't been to check?" Stefan shook his head. He hadn't wanted to go. He didn't know what he would say to his daughter. To him, she was a traitor. Her mother had died at the hands of Germans. And if his daughter hadn't sheltered Sara and kept her safe... each time he had such a thought a deep rage welled up within him making him want to hurt Klara if that were the case. "We should go immediately, come on." Pavel was already heading towards the door.

Ascending the stairs to Klara's apartment, neither spoke. The moment of truth was close at hand. Receiving no answer, Pavel turned the handle. The door opened, revealing an apartment which was immaculately clean and tidy but eerily quiet. There was nobody there.

"They've gone," uttered a small, wan face peeping around a doorjamb.

"Sarinka!" Stefan rushed to cuddle her. Now twelve she remained small, a delicate little thing who had never experienced the innocent happiness of childhood. A girl whose years had been spent in perpetual fear of discovery, daring to exist in a world that had decreed she was less than human.

"Where did they go?" asked Pavel.

"They didn't say. They left with Greta yesterday."

"Greta?"

"Their little girl." Stefan and Pavel exchanged looks. Stefan's was one of bewilderment, everything was happening so fast. Only yesterday he had thought he had no son, a daughter-in-law and a grandson in England who he had no way of contacting, and no idea that he had another grandchild. "They told me it would be safer for me to stay here and go to the police station to seek help, but I was too afraid to go outside. Where's Marta?"

"She… she had to go away," answered Stefan.

"And my parents, have they come back for me yet?"

"No, but they will, soon." Stefan knew that was almost certainly another lie but she looked so lost and vulnerable, he didn't have the heart to hit her with the truth. He took her hand. "Let's go back to my apartment."

"Can I bring my things?"

"Things?"

"Yes, all the lovely clothes and toys Klara and Jürgen bought for me."

As they walked back, Sara's hand squeezed Stefan's each time they saw a soldier and she turned her head in towards Stefan's side.

"It's all right, Sarinka. The Nazis have gone, gone for good. No one is going to hurt you or take you away."

The next morning when Stefan entered his workshop, the wooden faces lined up on the shelves no longer stared back reflecting emptiness. Yesterday had been an unexpected day, an incredible one. When he first awoke he had panicked, fearing it had been but a dream. He had been so convinced joy was a past emotion, one that wouldn't return. How wrong he had been, he smiled to himself.

Placing three recently finished puppets in his shoulder bag, Stefan set off across town to deliver them. People stood in small groups, chatting and laughing in the late spring sunshine. A few Soviet soldiers casually watched the world go by as they smoked and ogled the pretty maidens of Prague.

Approaching Strossmayer Square beyond Letna Park, Stefan could see the two fairytale like towers of the pseudo-gothic church of Saint Antonin of Padua, so similar in appearance to Prague's emblematic Tyn Church in the Old

Town Square. He gave thanks that his city had
survived virtually unscathed. So many of the
once beautiful cities of Europe now lay in ruins,
the architectural and artistic labours of centuries nothing more than mountains of rubble. So
much beauty destroyed.

Entering the square he stopped, observing many
huddled together, some seated on suitcases,
others sitting on the ground as if the rounding
up of the city's Jewish population was still continuing. Czech men with rifles guarded them,
while others walked around with buckets and
paint brushes putting white swastikas on their
backs.

"We're finally getting rid of the Germans in our
midst," said a virtually toothless old man next to
him. "They say all Czechs with German heritage
are going to be expelled."

"Oh." Stefan didn't volunteer an opinion but
the policy didn't disturb him. After all, German
Czechs had been trying to dismember Czechoslovakia since her birth. They would always hanker
after being part of Germany, better to send them
there so they could never cause any more trouble
was his view and that of the majority of Czechs.

He made his way across the square, passing the
group. A few metres ahead of him a young Czech
man was lunging at a woman, trying to pull her
out of the crowd. Her husband leapt to his feet to
protect her. The Czech thwacked him across the
face with his rifle and the man fell backwards

onto the ground.

"You filthy German pig!" The Czech already had his rifle pointed at him and appeared about to shoot.

"Stop!" shouted Stefan.

"What's it to you?" demanded the Czech, breathing heavily through his nostrils. "Are you a Nazi lover? Should I shoot you too?" He moved his gun and aimed at Stefan.

"No, I hate them. They murdered my wife. But the war's over, the killing has to stop."

The Czech glared at him for what seemed to Stefan a long time. The man's anger didn't appear to be abating. Stefan shouldn't have said anything. He wouldn't have said anything if it hadn't been him, but he had spared Stefan once.

"Hmm." The Czech grunted, lowered his rifle and spat at the man on the ground before walking away.

The woman held her two children close, her eyes still fearful. Rudi slowly got up, wiping blood from his mouth as he did so. He and Stefan stared at each other for a moment before Stefan continued on his way. Wandering home after making his delivery, Stefan wondered if the same fate had befallen Klara. She and Jürgen had protected Sara, they deserved to be safe.

CHAPTER 31

Klara and Jürgen were sitting in a cinema. Greta was on her father's knee. It was a theatre Klara and her husband had often come to, laughing as they watched German comedies and sometimes films in Czech, which the Nazis had permitted provided they had German subtitles and were apolitical.

Today they hadn't come to see a film. They hadn't wanted to be here at all. They had hoped to get out of the city unnoticed but they'd been stopped, and now they were with hundreds of others in darkness. They were more fortunate than some, they had seats. Many were on the floor, squashed next to one another.

Every so often light from bright flashlights would move along the walls and down the rows. But they weren't held by usherettes showing people to their seats. Instead, a Soviet soldier would come and grab a woman and take her away for a while.

German soldiers had raped countless women when they invaded Russia and murdered so many too. As far as the Russians were concerned, it was time for the Germans to know what that was like.

Whenever a beam of light travelled along her row, Klara slid down in her seat and buried her face in Jürgen's arm, hoping. She stuck out her fat belly. If the light stopped upon her maybe they would be repulsed by a heavily pregnant woman and choose someone else. She was lucky, her tactic worked.

Able to live in the light once more, Sara ran around the park on Petrin Hill her arms spread out wide with delight while Stefan and his son sat on the grass looking over the city bathing in the glow of the evening sun.

"Were you involved in killing Heydrich?" asked Stefan.

"In the planning, yes. I was extremely fortunate that the Nazis never knew about me. I spent the rest of the war in a safe house out in the country until we heard on the radio from the BBC that the Americans were near Prague. I broke cover then and returned to join the uprising."

"You deserve a medal."

"Hardly. Those who gave their lives for us are the real heroes."

"I was there when Heydrich was shot."

"You were there?" Pavel asked in disbelief.

"Yes, passing by. I'd been delivering ammo hidden in my old puppet theatre. I even got bullet holes in it during the shoot out between the resistance and Heydrich and his driver. I had to destroy it in case they came looking."

"Your smuggling of arms around the city has got to be worth a medal."

"I'd rather have your mother here than any medal."

"I know, me too. Have you thought what you'll do about Sara?"

"Keep her and look after her. Your mother and I made a promise to Matous and Raisa, a promise I intend to keep."

"Of course. Do you think they survived?"

"I doubt it."

Klara and her family spent more days locked in the cinema. In the pitch black, there was much time to think. She regretted that they had tried to flee as they did. She should first have taken Greta to her parents and asked them to look after her. Klara fretted what would happen when her baby was born. She didn't know where they would be and if they would be fed. If not, her milk would dry up and then... She emitted a groan of helplessness.

Klara wondered what her parents were doing now the war had ended. And Pavel. She hoped they had all lived. If they had, they would surely be celebrating like it was Christmas. Did they miss her or had she been forgotten? How she wished her mother and father could have met Jürgen. He had risked everything to hide Sara, treated her like his own daughter. Her family would never get to meet him, never get to know who he really was and why she loved him so.

Russian commands which she didn't understand interrupted her thoughts. She and Jürgen copied what others were doing and got up and slowly funnelled out into the bright light of a summer's day. It hurt their eyes after so long spent in darkness. In a long line, they were marched across town and up Pariszka. Once some of them had shopped at its luxurious boutiques or sat eating cake and drinking coffee in its swanky cafes, unaware or simply not caring that they were only metres away from Josefov and suffering. Bystanders watched them, some shouted insults. Klara felt slimy spittle land on her cheek and run down her face.

Crossing Cechuv bridge, they reached Letna Park and were directed into the sports stadium. Under the hot sun, people scrambled to claim a space for themselves on the baked mud and brown grass.

It was while a lightning storm raged above one night and large raindrops pounded the earth that Klara doubled up in pain. Her contractions had started. A couple of women nearby made Klara as comfortable as they could and stayed by her side while Jürgen and Greta moved a good distance away so that the little girl wouldn't be upset by her mother crying out in pain.

When the sun rose and leaving Greta with another family, Jürgen returned, keen to see his new child. Klara sat cradling the baby in her arms. His face fell. His wife's tears weren't ones of joy and his child's skin was pale with a purple tint to it. Before long someone alerted the authorities and two men arrived demanding the baby. Klara tried to stop them but they wrenched the corpse from her arms.

"You can't keep him any longer. Dead bodies spread disease."

For six weeks they lived under the hot sun, hungry and sunburned. By the time they were marched to the station, Klara had given up hope and was ready to accept death. Taken to Terezin, Klara thought the end had come when they were shoved into the showers on arrival and one woman shouted out "gas" and others screamed. But only cold water dribbled down.

Anxiety soared again when they were marched to the station and told to climb into wooden freight wagons without windows. Talk of death camps filled the cramped space. Klara held Greta tightly. When the train stopped everyone was ordered to disembark. They did so silently, climbing out reluctantly. Was this it? Would they be shot and buried in a mass grave?

"See that," shouted the officer in charge. It was no Auschwitz or Belsen but a landscape of green hills and meadows. "That's Germany. Go."

Nearly three million Germans were expelled from their homes in Czechoslovakia. It is thought about thirty thousand died before they reached Germany, either in revenge attacks or from their treatment in transit camps.

CHAPTER 32

The night that his daughter gave birth to his still-born grandson, Stefan's happiness reached new heights. Knocks on the door which he had once feared as portents of doom, had become occasions for celebration. The two men were pitifully thin, their cheeks sunken and their jackets hung from them as though they were coat hangers.

"Thank God, you're alive! Come in."

"Sarinka?" Matous asked softy as if frightened the answer would be what he most feared.

"She's just fallen asleep. Why don't you go wake her."

Neither Stefan or Pavel could hide their tears of joy as they heard Sara's cries of surprised delight coming from her bedroom. When Matous and his son emerged from the room after Sara had fallen back to sleep, Stefan had already laid bread, cheese and cold meat on the table together with two bottles of beer.

"Come eat."

"This must be most of your rations for the week," said Matous.

"No matter, you need it more." Stefan watched

with pleasure as they devoured nearly all the food he possessed.

"I can't thank you and Marta enough for saving Sarinka. Is Marta out?"

Stefan explained.

"I'm sorry, Stefan, she was such a wonderful person. I must go thank Klara and her husband. It's good to know that there were some Germans who didn't agree with the Nazis."

"You can't, they're gone. All Germans remaining have been rounded up and are being deported, including those who were born here. Have you had any word from Raisa?"

"No, she was put on a train with my mother to another camp. It would be a miracle if she has survived."

Stefan placed his hand on Matous' wrist. "My dear friend, I can't imagine what you and Jakub have endured."

"On the contrary, we were the lucky ones. Life in Terezin was hard, very hard, and many died there from disease and Nazi brutality but most were shipped off to the extermination camps, and they're the ones who won't be coming back. The barbarity of the Nazis is beyond comprehension."

"I know, all they did is only just beginning to come out. We hear of new horrors they committed on the radio on a daily basis."

"I'll never know for certain why Jakub and I managed to avoid transportation. We wouldn't be here tonight if we hadn't. I can only think it was because of an SS officer who had a passion for classical music. He had us go to their quarters every evening and play while he and other officers ate. We had to dress up in eighteenth century costumes and white wigs that he'd got for us. The Nazis' puppets, Jakub said. And we were, they pulled the strings and we danced to their tune. But it was a price worth paying to stay alive. Sometimes we would find it so hard to concentrate. The sight and smell of all that delicious food they dined on while we played was a torture in itself."

Yet as Matous had said, they had been lucky. Few of the over fifty thousand Jews living in Prague when the Nazis invaded survived the war.

"How did it end?" asked Stefan.

"It must have been early May. One day the SS fled. For a few days we could hear the noise of battle nearby and then the Soviets arrived. Typhoid broke out and we were all forbidden to leave and kept in quarantine for a couple of weeks. Again, we were lucky as we didn't catch it. Many did, they say over a thousand died from that outbreak. It's so sad after they had survived the Nazis that they should still not have made it. I'll forever be grateful to the Russians for liberating us. I hear they liberated Prague too."

"No, we the citizens rose up and kicked out the Germans. The Russians only turned up once they had gone. The Americans could have freed us earlier, which would have saved many lives, but the Russians insisted on being allowed to take Prague and the Americans held back to give them time to get here."

"That sounds like anti-Soviet propaganda to me. The Russians are our true friends, they won't abandon us when we need help in the future."

Stefan bit his tongue, a political argument wasn't appropriate this evening. The important thing was his best friend had lived and Sara had her father and brother back. "Have you thought about what you'll do? You're welcome to stay with us as long as you want. It might get a little crowded when Pavel's wife and son arrive from England but we'll manage somehow."

"Wife and son? Congratulations, Paja," said Matous. "I shall look forward to meeting your family. I appreciate your offer, Stefan. We'll stay here tonight and start looking tomorrow for a place to live. I'm hoping I'll be able to get my parents' house back. The Nazis or their supporters who would have got to live there will be gone."

"Do you think you'll rejoin the orchestra?" asked Stefan.

"No, after who we were forced to perform for I've lost all desire to play. It would only remind me of the past. I plan to involve myself in politics to ensure what has happened can never be repeated. And I can do it openly now that they've made the Communist Party legal once more."

Later in the year Susan and Stanislav arrived from England. Stefan liked Susan a great deal although they could only communicate through Pavel. She spoke no Czech and Stefan no English. Stanislav was young enough to pick up the new language from his father and grandfather with ease. An inquisitive child, he tottered up and down the stairs to visit his grandfather in his workshop with the jerky motions of a puppet. Stefan doted on his grandson, and didn't mind that he had to spend a considerable time each evening untangling the strings of puppets Stanislav had played with.

Pavel got his medal and also a job in the Foreign Ministry in the Cernin Palace working for the Foreign Minister, Jan Masaryk, son of the country's founder. Jan Masaryk had been a member of President Benes' government in exile in London during the war. Soon Pavel had the money to move his family to an apartment closer to his office. Yet Stefan's own apartment didn't revert to a place of doleful solitude. He had a family once more, and thoughts of them made him enjoy the sunshine streaming in through the windows which not so long ago he would have resented.

Stefan wondered if Klara and her family had made it to Germany and how they were surviving. He couldn't imagine that things would be easy there. Perhaps one day she would write and tell him. The ice in his heart was finally melting. At the end of the year, the Soviets withdrew from Prague and the rest of Czechoslovakia. Stefan was glad to see them go. They didn't exude the same menace as the Nazis, on the surface at least, but it was a relief to have the city finally free of foreign troops.

The Christmas season of 1945 was almost like old times. Pavel took a day off work to help his father with a puppet show in the Old Town Square. It was the first outing for the new mobile puppet theatre Stefan had constructed. A wheelwright he knew had made the wheels and Stefan had painted the theatre in red, white and blue to reflect the colours of Czechoslovakia's flag. No longer need he fear that the theatre would draw unwanted attention to him and risk his arrest.

On Christmas Eve, Stefan presented his grandson with his own miniature puppet set that he had made for him. The family attended midnight mass at Saint Nicholas. Stanislav spent the service fast asleep on his father's shoulder sucking his thumb and making endearing sniffling noises. To Stefan, it felt that God had finally returned to Prague.

On New Year's day, the family were invited to Matous' home. He had secured the return of the family home on Kampa Island. Radmila was there to greet them.

"Isn't she lovely?" said Matous as she went

around the drawing room filling the adults' wine glasses.

"Indeed," replied Stefan.

"We're engaged."

"Engaged?" Stefan couldn't hide his surprise and didn't offer his congratulations. "What if Raisa is still alive?"

"We had word last month that she and my mother were gassed in Belsen."

"That's terrible, so awful. I was very fond of her. Marta was too."

"So was I but our marriage had run its course long ago."

"Isn't it all a bit soon?"

"Not really. Life is short and, as we've both ex-perienced, hangs by a thread. You need to seize the moment. It won't come around again."

"What about your children?"

"They are fine about it. They say all they want is for me to be happy. You and I are blessed to have survived and to have our families. And I have yet more good news. I have been chosen by the Party to stand for Parliament in this year's elections."

"Well, I won't be voting for you."

"You'll change your mind once we have a Com-munist government, and you see what a differ-ence it makes to the lives of the workers. Come, lunch is ready. Radka is an excellent cook, even with the limited ingredients you can get these days."

At the dinner table, Stefan noticed Jakub and

Sara spoke little. They appeared to be sitting under their own low cloud of grey. They might not object to their father's forthcoming marriage but Stefan understood how they must miss the all encompassing love that was their mother. He still missed Marta and how her love had nurtured the entire family.

Unlike his brother and sister, Yosef was animated and excited to talk of his time in the Soviet army. Matous listened with approval. It seemed that their shared enthusiasm for Communism had created a bond which had previously been lacking.

"And you, Pavel, were you brainwashed by the Americans and British that the Soviets are to be feared?" asked Yosef.

"Not at all, I am perfectly capable of making my own assessment," replied Pavel abruptly.

"And exactly what is your assessment?"

"That Czechoslovakia should be left free to chart her own course, dominated by no one."

"That's naive, a small country like ours needs a strong ally we can rely upon. You saw what happened when we didn't."

"Yet another foreign power controlling our destiny you mean, because that's what Communism would result in."

"There's a change for the better coming, and those who stand in its way will be swept aside," retorted Yosef.

"That sounds no different to what the Nazis

would have said."

"How dare you!" Yosef rose swiftly from his chair.

"That's enough from both of you," intervened Stefan. "No more talk of politics. Let's enjoy this wonderful meal."

But the barriers had been raised. The remainder of the meal passed in an awkward conversation of superficial remarks of little consequence.

Walking home, Stefan couldn't help wondering if he was gradually losing his best friend.

CHAPTER 33

It was spring when another person re-entered Stefan's life, a bunch of sweet smelling flowers in her hand.

"I brought these for Marta," announced Dagmar. "I wanted to thank you both again and let you know that I'm okay."

"She would have loved them but she's no longer with us, the Germans murdered her."

Dagmar looked genuinely sad. "I'm so sorry, Stefan. I admired her a great deal."

"Won't you come in?"

"No, thank you, I'm in a rush. I'm standing for Parliament once more. Hopefully I'll beat the Communist candidate. If they ever manage to get hold of the reigns of power, they won't ever let them go. I hear that your friend, Matous, is standing for them in another part of the city."

"Yes, but my vote will be going to your party."

"I'm glad to hear it."

"Dagmar, can we-"

"No, Stefan," said Dagmar anticipating what he wished to say. "It's time to move on, not revisit the past. Here, take these flowers, I don't suppose you ever buy any."

She thrust them into Stefan's hand and hurried down the stairs before he could say anything, a butterfly who didn't wish to be caught in anyone's net.

Come the elections of May 1946, Dagmar and Matous both won their seats. Overall the Communists scored the biggest vote, but with only thirty-eight percent they were obliged to form a coalition. Their leader, Klement Gottwald, became Prime Minister. Yet within a year the Communists' popularity had already plummeted, and it seemed likely their share of the vote in the elections due in May 1948 would tumble and they would be out of government. With Russian help, the Czechoslovak Communist Party began planning to stop that happening.

In February 1948, with the aim of bringing down the government, non-Communist government ministers resigned in protest at the replacement of police chiefs with loyal Communists, hoping to persuade the President to sack the government and force early elections. Stefan sat glued to his radio each day listening to developments.

Large numbers of Communist supporters and their militias were out on the streets each day, intimidating any who didn't share their beliefs. It felt as if democracy was once again close to collapse. Concerned, Stefan went out into a grey snowy morning and headed to the Old Town

Square. A massive crowd of enthusiastic Communist supporters filled the huge space, several holding the red flags of the Czechoslovak Communist Party which displayed both the Czechoslovak flag and the yellow Soviet hammer and sickle.

The object of their attention was the rococo Kinsky Palace. Curious, Stefan pushed his way forward through a sea of black overcoats to get a closer look. A deafening roar rang out, greeting the arrival on the balcony of Gottwald and other prominent communists in their Russian winter hats. Amongst them Stefan spotted Matous, who would soon be appointed Minister of Culture. To wild cheering, Gottwald proclaimed the establishment of a Communist state.

Fearing Russian intervention and a civil war, President Benes had acceded to Gottwald's demands. A Communist coup had become a fait accompli, and Czechoslovakia had become the last piece of the Russian jigsaw to fall into place, completing a line of Soviet satellite states in Europe from Poland in the north to Bulgaria in the south.

In a state of disbelief, Stefan wandered despondently back home. How could it be that Prague was once more under a dictatorship and foreign control, this time the Russians? Yet again the silent majority had been caught napping, their chance to save their country already gone.

Pavel too feared for the future, even more so only two weeks later. Susan was surprised to see him arrive home at ten in the morning.

"You look unwell. Are you feeling ill?"

"Something terrible has happened. Jan Masaryk, the Foreign Minister, is dead."

"Dead?"

"Yes, his body was found in the courtyard at the Foreign Ministry first thing this morning. The Communists are saying he committed suicide. I don't believe that, not for one moment. He was the only non-Communist Minister left. They must have pushed him out of the window. A defenestration, just like when religious bigots would hurl their opponents out of the high windows at the castle in times gone by."

"What happens now?" asked Susan.

"We pack and take a train out of the country while we still can. I don't want our son growing up under this regime."

Susan wasn't unhappy to hear they were to leave Prague. She couldn't deny the city's architectural charm, but she continued to struggle with the language and it wasn't home to her.

"But what about your father? We can't abandon him."

"I'll go on down there and ask him to leave with us. I'll take the big suitcase and you bring what you can carry in the smaller one and meet us at the station, under the clock."

Stefan didn't wait for Pavel to explain the reason for his visit when his son burst into the workshop.

"I have some good news, Paja," he said. "Klara has written. They are safe and living in Munich and want to come visit us. She doesn't know about your mother yet, that will come as a shock."

"I doubt they'll be allowed to visit. There's talk of the borders with the West being closed at any moment. Jan Masaryk, my boss, is dead. I'm convinced he was murdered. Susan and I are leaving the country while it's still possible to do so. We want you to come too. We can all go to England."

Stefan's face was impassive. "I'll help you pack your things and we'll meet Susan and Stanislav at the station. Come on, let's go upstairs and get what you need."

Stefan didn't move. "I can't, not at my time of life. I've always lived in Prague. I couldn't live anywhere else, I'd be too homesick. Anyway, I'd only slow you down."

"But we might never see you again."

"Don't say that. The Nazis were only here for six years, the Communists won't last."

"What will you do?"

"What I've always done. I'll be fine. You don't need to worry about me, focus on your family. I'll go up to your place later and bring back anything that looks like you would have wanted to take with you but couldn't and keep it safe here for your return. Now go, you mustn't keep them waiting. Give me a hug, and make sure you write this time."

That evening Stefan blinked repeatedly in quick succession as bitter tears stung his eyes while he held his daughter's letter in one hand and a picture of Pavel and his family in the other. Less than three years after hope had blossomed once more, the frost of a bitter winter had killed it and it felt like spring might never come again.

CHAPTER 34

"Where's your father?" asked Susan when Pavel arrived at the station.

"He wouldn't come."

"I don't want to go without him." Stanislav stamped his feet with defiance.

"We'll see him soon. We're going on an adventure, and you can tell him all about it when we next see him. I need to buy our tickets."

"To where?" whispered Susan, not wishing to attract her son's attention who was now absorbed watching a train arrive.

"Vienna, it's our only option. Dresden is in the Soviet zone of Germany, and Hungary and Poland would be no better. Vienna is jointly controlled by the Russians and the Western Allies. It's our best chance."

The two adults walked to the platform with churning stomachs, each holding one of their son's hands as he hopped, skipped and jumped between them like a human yoyo, not a care in the world. The ticket inspector waved them through the gate. They boarded and chose a carriage which was almost empty. Pavel wiped his clammy hands against his coat as they sat down. He didn't know what would happen at the border.

The journey passed more quickly than he thought it would. Stanislav entertained them with his excited reactions when he spotted cows and horses and castles and churches from the train window. The countryside looked idyllic in the purity of its whiteness. The snow hadn't been crushed underfoot into an cheerless slush as in Prague.

As they neared the border, Pavel suggested they get something to eat. Reaching the toilet, he ushered his wife and son in, leaving the door slightly ajar in the hope of not arousing suspicion.

"What's happening?" asked Stanislav.

"We're playing hide and seek. If we're not found, you get to choose a new toy. Do you think you can be quiet until I say so?" His boy nodded enthusiastically.

The train came to a halt. "Papers," a harsh voice called out. Pavel picked up his son and held him close. The family had squashed themselves into the tiny space behind the door. So long as no one came in and closed the door, they shouldn't be seen. Footsteps approached ever closer until they stopped right outside.

The door was casually kicked open. Pavel's heart was in his mouth. The footsteps resumed.

"He didn't find us, Tatka," whispered Stanislav.

"Just a few minutes more and we will have won,"

said his father.

When the train laboriously began to chug forwards, the adults traded smiles of success. They were out of Czechoslovakia.

"When can I choose my toy?" asked their son as they returned to their seats.

"Once we get to Vienna."

Arriving in Vienna was exhilarating. Stefan and Susan walked with a new found confidence along the platform and through the smoke floating from the train, a confidence which proved to be misplaced when they emerged from the cloud.

"Papiere," demanded a man in uniform. Although he asked in German, the red star on his hat provided a confirmation Pavel had fervently hoped wouldn't be the case.

Within hours, Pavel and his family, unable to produce an exit visa, were on a train back to Prague. Armed guards were positioned at either end of the carriage. A handful of others who had somehow also made it across the border, were sitting dejectedly. Pavel could almost taste the atmosphere of fearful anticipation.

"What about my toy?" complained Stanislav.

"We'll get it when we're back in Prague," said his mother, concealing her own concern about what would happen to them now. Her mind bombarded her with awful thoughts. The worst of which was that they would be imprisoned and their son taken away from them. This time they barely acknowledged Stanislav's almost constant commentary of what he could see outside.

Only after the rest of the train had disembarked were those in this carriage of doom permitted to alight. Each small group was escorted away separately by uncommunicative men in civilian clothes whose body language was decidedly hostile. Pavel and his family were taken to a black car outside and driven off at speed. At their destination, they were bundled out and into an austere building of dark stone with bars at the windows. Once inside, Pavel was pulled away from his family by two men who ignored Stanislav's cries for his father. Taken to a windowless room with a single light bulb hanging like a noose from the ceiling, he was left alone to fret what might be happening to Susan and Stanislav, and to try to come up with an explanation. It must have been more than an hour before he heard the jangle of a key being inserted in the lock. Two men in sombre suits and ties and white shirts which were sallow with age entered. Pavel recognised one of them and rose from his chair.

"Yosef, thank God it's you. This is all a terrible mistake. I was scared, I-"

"Sit down. And it's Comrade Rubinstein." The response was unfriendly, cold as a strong north wind in winter. "Exactly what were you scared of, Janicek?"

"That I would be blamed for the Foreign Minister's death."

"Why would that be? Are you guilty of murder?"

"No, of course not but I worked closely with him, and I was first in the office that awful day it happened."

"Mmm." Yosef's response was non-committal.

"What about my wife and child?"

"They're being looked after."

"Where?"

"Let's focus on what you did, then we can talk about them."

"But I didn't do anything," protested Pavel. Yosef ignored him while he offered a cigarette to his colleague, who was short yet stocky like a boar. His sharp tusks were his pencil and notebook. He was able to wound Pavel by writing whatever suited the secret police. Yosef exhaled and blew smoke across the table directly into Pavel's face.

"I don't think you killed Masaryk."

Pavel relaxed a little. "I was stupid. I panicked unnecessarily, I'm sorry, Comrade Rubinstein."

"You have an interesting background. Running off to fight for the English."

"I wanted to do my bit for our country, like you did. You already know that."

"The difference is those who went to the West were corrupted. They returned as counter revolutionaries. We know that you were spying for the British."

Pavel sat up sharply, astonished by the absurdity of the accusation.

"Absolutely not. I would never do such a thing. I would never betray my homeland."

"Of course you're going to deny it. Taking an English wife and coming back to Prague so you could work together."

"That's not true."

"The penalty for treason is death," pronounced Yosef with something close to relish. "Do you want your wife to be hanged, and your son sent to a state orphanage, growing up knowing that both his parents were traitors. Imagine the effect on him, on his future prospects, a life ruined before it has barely begun. However, if you were to confess, I can promise you that your wife would be freed and your son would get to stay with her." He stood up. "My generous offer expires in an hour. I expect you need time to think so we'll leave you in peace."

Pavel placed his arms on the table and laid his head upon them, his mind peering into a void. He had never expected this. Guilty of attempting to emigrate illegally, yes. Maybe a few years in jail at worst but not espionage. Feeling nauseous, he had nothing on which to vomit. It had been so long since he had last eaten. This was checkmate, Pavel was beaten. All he could influence was the fate of his wife and son.

"I'll confess," he volunteered immediately the two harbingers of death returned. "But how do I know you'll keep your promise."

"When we're finished here, I'll let you watch them leave. They're of no interest to me. My work today will earn me a nice promotion, I have no reason to harm them," said Yosef.

Pavel wanted to grab the bastard by the throat, kill him as he had been trained to do but that would only ensure his family suffered. Instead, he made up a convoluted story about how he had worked for MI6 and passed confidential information obtained through his job at the Foreign Ministry to the British Embassy.

"That wasn't so hard, was it?" Yosef's tone was self-satisfied. "Once it's typed up, we'll be back for your signature. Meanwhile I'll have some food sent in."

Pavel forced himself to eat the hard stale bread and lump of cheese. He dipped the bread in his water to soften it enough to make it edible. He chewed lethargically as he wondered whether his family would be allowed a final visit, and how long it would be until they tightened that coarse rope around his neck and he was left kicking the air, seeking a foothold which didn't exist. No, he reprimanded himself, don't let them steal the days that remain, think only of good memories, of family and friends, of Stanislav's chuckle and Susan's love.

Pavel didn't bother to read the confession before he signed it, there was no point. Escorted out of the room and into the corridor he was taken to a window. Yosef's sidekick sloped off and two men waited.

"Look, there they go," said Yosef.

Through the bars and a mist of tears, Pavel

watched his wife and son walk down the street lit by lamplight. Susan looked back once towards the building. Pavel raised his hand but she turned away, their eyes never connecting. She hadn't seen him and disappeared into the shadows with his boy.

CHAPTER 35

"Is Paja not with you?" asked Stefan when his daughter-in-law and grandson arrived at his apartment. "I thought you were all leaving together."

"Stanicek, why don't you play with those toys your grandfather has brought down from our place," said Susan noticing them in the corner of the room next to other belongings of theirs. Once he was engrossed in his game, Susan explained as well as she could in her halting Czech all that had happened.

Stefan sank onto a dining chair, overwhelmed by the news. "I don't believe for a moment he's a spy. They've forced him to admit to something he hasn't done. They probably blackmailed him, threatening not to let you go unless he signed a confession." Stefan rubbed the finger tips of one hand against his forehead, seeking inspiration. He knew what happened to those deemed guilty of espionage. The answer came to him and he dropped his hand. "I will go visit Matous. He's a minister in the government and should be able to help us."

"Do you think so?" Susan seized the idea, felt it infuse her exhausted self with the rush of hope. "I'll go to his house this evening."

It was Sara who answered the door. She had emerged from her chrysalis into a striking teenager, similar in many ways to Raisa when Stefan had first made her acquaintance in Siberia thirty years ago, although Sara's features were more delicate than her mother's had been.

"He's out attending a concert at Obecni Dum, entertaining a delegation from Moscow," she said in response to Stefan's question.

Head down, he walked quickly over Charles Bridge and through the Old Town.

Next to the Powder Tower so blackened with soot, lounged the sandstone hue of the city's Art Nouveau masterpiece and an ebullient celebration of what the twentieth century had promised in its early years. Finished when Stefan was only fifteen and when it had seemed as though life would always be light and breezy, Obecni Dum looked like a piece of Paris supplanted to Prague with its allegorical statuary and glass cupola. The enchantment continued inside with marble everywhere, pendulant chandeliers, and circular glass ceilings of vibrant colours.

So often as he'd passed it, Stefan had admired this striking edifice, one which wasn't entangled in the city's often violent history. Tonight he gave it scant attention. Enquiring at the foyer, he went up the wide staircase. From the Smetana Concert Hall boomed the victorious last few bars of Tchaikovsky's 1812 Overture, commemorating the defeat of Napoleon's army in Russia. It now served also as a celebration of Russia's victory over Nazi Germany and a reminder that Russia was unbeatable. Straight-backed waiters stood against a wall of the reception area, holding trays sparkling with glasses of Russian champagne. Soon the privileged of this new order would emerge from the concert, unctuously fawning before their Soviet masters.

As if consumed by stage fright, Stefan departed hurriedly. Tonight was certainly not the best time. Whatever had he been thinking? Accosting Matous in front of Stalin's delegation would be disastrous. Stefan called again at Kampa Island, and Sara confirmed that her father should be at home the following evening.

Since the end of the war, the once close friends had been drifting apart as slowly but as irrevocably as the ice breaking up on the Vltava. To rise through the ranks of the Party, an ambitious person couldn't allow sentimentalities from the past to threaten his ascent. Matous had asked an important Party official to be his best man when he married Radmila. Stefan knew from that point on his refusal to hug the Russian bear would forever alter things between them. Yet he had high hopes that Matous would do him one last favour.

The next morning, Susan walked her father-in-law to the building where she had last seen her husband. As they approached it, Stefan experienced an involuntary shudder as if an icicle was being run along his spine. He had been here before as a prisoner himself. Worse still, it was almost certainly where Marta had met her death. The Nazis may have gone but terror and persecution still thrived in that gruesome place.

The guard at the door thrust his right hand out and told them to go before Stefan could complete his sentence.

"I won't warn you again," he said when Stefan tried to finish his request to be allowed to see his son.

Susan took his arm and pulled. "Come, we should go."

That evening when Stefan arrived, Matous took him straight to his study. A large photograph of Gottwald and Stalin shaking hands, with Matous clearly visible amongst those clapping in the background, hung on the wall behind his desk.

"Sara said you would be coming, do take a seat. I would offer you a drink but I am always so busy these days and have a lot to get through this evening."

"I'll get straight to the point then." Stefan strained to keep curtness from his voice, annoying Matous wouldn't advance his cause. "Pavel has been arrested and accused of spying for the British. They've forced a confession out of him. It's a fabrication and I need you to intervene."

Matous sat back in his chair and folded his arms. "I can't do as you ask. If he is innocent our legal system will establish that. Justice must be allowed to take its course."

"Justice, is that what you call it? How would you feel if it were Jakub? I'm begging you, Matous, please. If our friendship meant anything to you, if our saving Sara from the Nazis-"

Matous unfolded his arms. "Stop. I'll see what I can do but I can make no promises. Come see me this time next Thursday."

Stefan stood to leave. "I don't understand why you support them. They despise the Jews, surely you know that."

"Any dislike they may have for Jews is inconsequential compared to that of the Nazis or the anti-semitism of most Czechs for that matter. The Party doesn't dislike Judaism any more than it dislikes Catholicism or Protestantism. Religion has been such a source of hatred and conflict, a means of oppressing the masses for centuries. The Party doesn't believe in any religion and nor do I. I may have been born a Jew but I didn't choose to be one, and I no longer identify as one. I am an atheist now. We will build a good life for the workers here on earth, not deceive them with a promise that their suffering is to be endured because of a non-existent paradise that awaits them on death. I hope one day you will see the light, and understand that what we are creating is for the better."

Stefan held his tongue. Pavel's freedom was more important than an argument which would do nothing to change Matous' opinions. Yet the contradictions of Communism were as great as those of any other dictatorship. Matous lived in a grand house that could easily accommodate three families while they confiscated the property of the 'bourgeoisie', many of whom had lived in much more modest homes than Matous and other prominent Communists now got to enjoy.

The week passed interminably slowly. Stefan had told Susan that his meeting had gone extremely well to give her some respite from the torment which she must be suffering. Alone in his workshop, he bit his nails to the quick.

"I have good news," said Matous when Stefan presented himself the following Thursday.

"Oh thank you," Stefan exhaled in grateful relief.

"The charges are to be changed, there will be no execution, merely a spell of imprisonment."

"But-" Stefan had assumed Matous' 'good news' meant the charges were to be dropped in their entirety.

"Your son is a very lucky man to escape with his life, be thankful," said Matous noticing the initial look of joy disappear from Stefan's face.

"How long a sentence will he get?"

"That will be for the judge to decide. It's fortunate my son, Yosef, was the investigating officer."

"Yosef?" Anger rose up within Stefan like boiling water spilling over a saucepan. "You mean your own son made up a pack of lies which he coerced my son into signing, and yet you take Yosef's side instead of demanding he tell the truth."

"I did the best we could."

"No, being complicit in executing or imprisoning those who have done no wrong and whose only crime is to want a free society, that is not doing the best you can."

Nostrils flaring, Matous stood up from his chair. "You need to leave."

"I'm glad to." Stefan stormed out. His friendship with Matous had gone cold like an old grave stone to the touch. The man cared more about his own advancement than the difference between right and wrong, and more than helping his oldest friend.

The judge's words "ten years' hard labour" hit as hard as a rock hurled with force. Pavel was led quickly away and denied the opportunity to speak to his family. Stefan held Susan as she sobbed without noise, her body convulsing against his.

CHAPTER 36

The guard who processed Pavel on his arrival at Jachymov, a spa town in the hilly northwest of the country near the German border, had a sadistic smirk on his face. "You might think you're a lucky bastard, but after a month here you'll be wishing they'd hung you instead."

Outside the town was the labour camp where Pavel would live, and the nearby mine where he would work. Started by the Nazis, the camp was being replenished with political prisoners to replace German prisoners of war who were now few in number.

Two barbed wire fences surrounded the camp huts. At night, the space between them was illuminated by blindingly bright searchlights shone from six machine gun towers. It was known as the death strip, because that is what awaited any who made a break for it and got trapped there.

First the Nazis and now the Soviets wanted uranium from the mine for their nuclear projects, and forced prison labour was the only way to get it out of the ground. No free man would sign up to endure the conditions and damage to their well-being the mining entailed.

When Pavel first entered the mine, his already low mood plumbed new depths. It was like an ogre's cave, a perpetual darkness that was seemingly infinite. The mine's dank shafts and corridors hacked into existence by those who had gone before him were a maze of horror lit only by the inadequate glow of the miners' headlamps. Ever farther into the belly of the earth they had to go, often six hundred metres or more underground as the seams nearer to the entrance had become exhausted. With picks and shovels, they were expected to dislodge chunks from the rock face and heft them into metal containers for their journey to the surface. Serious accidents and deaths from rock falls were a regular occurrence.

The working day began at five in the morning with only coffee and a piece of bread. Some days roll call outside in the elements could last for hours and would be repeated again come evening. Thirst was a constant. The men were only given a single cup of water per shift. Pavel soon joined the others open mouthed, waiting for a drop of water to fall from the rock ceiling above or licking it as it ran down the walls. Most of the time they were working knee deep in dirty water, and before long the skin on Pavel's feet was peeling off like soft bark from a tree.

After eight hours underground, a further three hours had to be endured at the surface sorting and cleaning rocks which had been mined.

Evenings offered political indoctrination, and a considerable chunk of their minimal wages was withheld as 'donations' to the Party. Russian personnel were in evidence everywhere. At the time, it was their only source of uranium in their race to match America and build nuclear bombs.

Pavel wondered how he could possibly survive ten years in such conditions. He soon came to realise that he wasn't supposed to. Most never made it out alive. The authorities found it cheaper to bring in new prisoners to take the place of those who died rather than devote resources to the welfare of those already here.

Packages couldn't be received and a postcard home could be sent or received only once every six months. Pavel had been sucked into a living hell.

In Prague, Stefan wondered if he would soon lose his grandson too. For some considerable time after the trial he said nothing about the matter. Emotions were too raw and the full implications of Pavel's conviction when they gradually became apparent were more than enough for his daughter-in-law to cope with.

Susan and Stanislav were thrown out of the apartment she and Pavel had lived in, and Susan received notification that she was to work as a street cleaner. Those related to enemies of the State were assigned menial jobs. She would be in good company, university professors and other intelligentsia would be amongst her co-workers as they swept the streets.

Nearing retirement age and doing a job which was considered to be an acceptable part of Czech culture, Stefan was permitted to continue making his puppets and give shows.

Stefan looked after Stanislav when he wasn't at school. When the boy grew, he too would find his options limited. A place at university for the son of a political prisoner would be out of the question. The stain of Pavel's 'crime' would forever be indelibly ingrained into the fabric of the Janiceks, their files at the StB, the secret police, prominently marked as a family that could never be trusted.

Stanislav was asleep in bed and Susan struggling to keep her eyes open as she lounged in an armchair, relieved to take the weight off her feet after another day of cleaning the city streets. The only good thing to have come from Susan's work was that talking with her fellow cleaners had vastly improved her ability to speak Czech.

"I would understand if you wanted to return to England with Stanicek," said Stefan, opposite her in the other armchair, both threadbare from too many years of use. "It might make sense. Maybe when Pavel is released they will deport him and you can all be together again and live in freedom."

"I can't say I haven't thought about it, life here is

nothing like I'd imagined it would be. But what if when Pavel's released they don't let him leave the country or allow me to come back? Or if I try and go to England, who's to say they won't throw me out but not allow Stanicek to come with me. It's a risk I dare not take."

"Paja's fortunate to have you for a wife," smiled Stefan. "You should go to bed, you look exhausted."

Susan lay down next to her son, breathing in the scent of the soap she had used to wash his face with that evening. It reminded her of roses and an English summer. As a street cleaner, her summer days were an unpleasant thing, smelling of sweat and tasting of grit. Exhausted she might be but she couldn't sleep. Like every night, she lay staring at the ceiling for a long time worrying about how her husband was coping. Her days might be hard but they were surely easy compared to what he must be going through.

Susan thought how different their lives would have been if only he had returned to England at the end of the war. They would all be together, perhaps in a small house with a garden and and a baby brother or sister for Stanislav. Susan imagined a thatched cottage down a leafy lane, their golden retriever chasing Stanislav around a garden blooming with wildflowers, and Pavel smiling at her as he held their new born daughter. How wonderful that would have been compared to their awful reality. She felt like weeping.

Buck up, Susan told herself. It was no good being maudlin. She had to be strong for her son and do the best she could until Pavel finally came home. Then they might be free to go to England and live the life they wanted, and if not they would make do with a life in Prague. All that really mattered was being a family again. Where was a secondary consideration.

Down in his workshop, Stefan fought the regime in the only way he knew how to as he put the finishing touches to his latest two puppets, ones that he couldn't sell and would only be able to use when confident that his audience were of a like mind. He made a large dimple in the chin of one and then began painting the two men. Onto the puppet without the dimple he brushed a thick, bushy moustache. Anyone but a cloistered monk would recognise them instantly, the two men who had made puppets of the citizens of Prague and forced them to dance to whatever tone deaf tune they composed.

Each time Stefan did a show, he would carefully survey those gathered. If satisfied that there was no one watching who looked like a secret police-man, he would take out Stalin and Gottwald and use them as if they were the village idiots to roars of laughter from an appreciative crowd.

It was already December when Susan ran into Stefan's workshop waving a plain postcard in her hand.

"I've heard from Pavel. He's all right." She held it

out for Stefan to read.

"Isn't it in English?"

"No, I expect the authorities wouldn't allow that. Go ahead, read it."

"My dearest Susan, I have been here several months now. It's much better than expected and I am doing well. How are you and Stanicek and Tatka? I miss you and love you all."

"That's wonderful news," said Stefan.

"Isn't it just, the best Christmas present."

Stefan hadn't the heart to tell her that he didn't believe Pavel's encouraging words. His son was doubtless trying to spare them further worry.

Come Christmas, the family didn't go to midnight mass. Secret police stood by church entrances taking note of those who still clung to the old ways.

CHAPTER 37

In the prison camp, Christmas day was the same as any other. Another day of misery with nothing to look forward to except sleep when Pavel wouldn't be conscious of his daily life. Though some nights even sleep brought him no peace as he dreamed of working in the mine or being back in Prague where his family would pass him by on the street, not hearing his shouts or seeing him.

Pavel recalled the words of the guard who had greeted him when he first arrived. The man was right, being hung would have been preferable to this existence.

Pavel was taken by surprise when a man barrelled into him and shoved him hard. "Move!"

The man fell on top of him as the roof of the tunnel collapsed nearby in a bomb of rock and dust.

"Are you all right?" asked the man when he got off Pavel.

"Yes, I think so," he coughed. "And you?"

"No worse than normal. Come on, we should start digging our way out. We can't rely on anyone else doing it for us."

Sick of the wretchedness of life in the mines, a

voice inside Pavel told him not to bother. Why try and get out just so he could be sent under the earth again. For a lot of the year he hardly saw daylight and rarely felt the sun on his face to remind him that he was still alive. In their small space, the oxygen wouldn't last long. At last, he could lie down and let death wrap him in her blanket where he could sleep and never be woken again to labour like a slave.

"Go ahead if you want, I don't care."

The man crouched down next to him. He looked older than his father but may not have been. After a few months in the mines, every prisoner aged well beyond their years. It was as if the dirt and dust wore away their skin, engraving deep creases in their faces.

"Listen, I've been here for over three years now. Next week they're setting me free so I am not giving up. They imprisoned me after the war because they say I'm a German even though I was born in Prague. I'll be deported to Germany but I'll get to see my family. And you, don't you have family, a reason to live."

"Yes, a wife and a boy. But I can't take this anymore, I just can't." Pavel's shoulders crumpled as he broke down, the pain coming out in pitiful sobs. The man put his arm around him.

"Let it out. It's okay. I understand. We've all felt like that but don't let the bastards win, don't give them that satisfaction. What's your name?"

"Pavel Janicek."

"I had a friend once with that surname. Stefan. He lived just off Nerudova in Prague, he made puppets."

"That's my father."

"Well, I'll be damned. I'm Rudi, Rudi Vogel. Your father saved my life once, twice in fact, so it's time for me to return the favour. Stay there if you don't feel up to it but I'm going to get us out of here or die in the attempt."

Rudi began clawing at the rocks with his bare hands. It wasn't many minutes until Pavel joined him. Although they worked for hours, they made little impact other than to create a tiny space through which oxygen could flow. Exhausted, Pavel took a rest. Rudi refused to stop, driven by determination to get out and get home. Yet come morning, the rock wall remained as impregnable as before.

They both sat on the hard, unyielding ground. Rudi slammed his fist down upon it, frustrated and demoralised.

"Hey, can you hear that?" said Pavel through lips as dry as desert sand.

It was the noise of footsteps. Near or far they couldn't tell. Sound echoed around this underground labyrinth. Their first call for help was a strangled croak but the next and the following were stronger. Getting a response, they hugged with delight.

Within a few hours they were able to wriggle out. Pavel got to spend a few days lying on his bed. He never saw Rudi again.

Pavel's initial euphoria at surviving didn't last more than a few days back in the mine. He was still as trapped as he had been with Rudi. Pavel hoped the next rock fall would kill him.

In Prague, like the tentacles of an octopus, Communism reached into every corner of life. Out in the suburbs, new towers were hastily erected, brutalist concrete apartment blocks for a workers' paradise as if ugly new city walls encircling the city. Many traditions were swept aside. Radio Prague's familiar call sign from Dvorak's New World Symphony was replaced by the Communist anthem, "Left foot forwards, left foot forwards, and never a backwards step!" Stefan leapt up and switched off the radio in disgust each time it was played.

Once more like he had done under the Nazis, he put away his medal and Legionnaire's uniform. There would be no further commemorations, no annual marches of proud men, proud to have won freedom for their country, men who were now ageing fast. The Prague bridge, Most Legii, named after the Legion had its name altered once again as it had been under the Nazis. The only place remaining where the Legion was commemorated was at a bank founded by returning Legionnaires, a rondo-cubist building erected in the 1920s. A marble frieze on the smoky red exterior depicted the Legionnaires' epic journey across Siberia.

What freedom had been like was gradually receding from the nation's collective memory, and the Legionnaires' fight against the Bolsheviks was something that the country's Soviet masters definitely wanted to erase from public consciousness.

Stanislav was learning Russian at school, it was compulsory. The boy was soon swept up in the new order, one which saw children as cementing its future, those who hadn't experienced the 'before'.

"Our teacher told us today that Jezisek, who once brought our presents, has grown into Grandfather Frost, whose path is lit not just by one star but a whole sky of red stars," he announced the moment he got home, his face glowing with the excitement at imparting the news and waiting for adult approval.

"That's what Russians believe. In England, we believe in Father Christmas who lives at the North Pole, but in Prague we have Jezisek," said his mother.

"Not any more." Stanislav stuck his chin out with certainty.

"But what if they're wrong? If you stop believing in Jezisek, there might be no presents at Christmas." Susan could see doubt appear in the boy's eyes. "But we should keep Jezisek our special secret. What do you say?"

Stanislav nodded.

"They're going to brainwash the young, and make our country a little Russia," bemoaned Stanislav to Susan once his grandson was in bed. "It breaks my heart what has happened to us."

Susan looked up from the sweater she was knitting her son for Christmas. "He brought home a letter yesterday inviting him to join the Young Pioneers now that he's eight."

"Hmm. Turn them into little automatons, that's what they want. It reminds me of the German Czech boys marching through Prague dressed in their Hitler Youth uniforms during the occupation."

"I'm not sure it's a breeding ground for evil like the Hitler Youth was. It says they will learn to be good citizens, learn to clean things and help old people. And they have summer camps which Stanicek would love. I was chatting about it in the queue for meat today with another woman. She says she got her children to join because if they stay in it and then join the Czechoslovak Youth Union when they reach fifteen, their prospects of getting into university or better jobs are much improved."

"Have you forgotten his father's been convicted of spying?"

"We can't change that but this might help, and Stanicek is keen to join. All his school friends are. Would you object?"

"You're his mother and you should decide, it's not my place to interfere. But be careful you don't lose your son to them. The State is seeking to break down the barriers between home and state and take away our right to privacy and family life."

Such thoughts didn't concern Stanislav when he came home in his Pioneer uniform of red neck tie, light blue shirt and dark blue trousers, his face sparkling like sunshine on water.

"Why, look at you," said his mother, disguising her misgivings about whether she'd done the right thing under a cheerful smile.

"Look, this is our salute," said her son placing the fingers of his right hand against his forehead. "It means a Pioneer is always thinking of how to help working people in all six continents. Do you want to know our motto?"

Susan nodded without much enthusiasm.

"Our group leader asks 'Are you ready for building and defending your socialist country?' And we shout back 'We are always ready'."

"Oh."

Stefan, who was standing outside his grandson's field of vision, rolled his eyes.

"Go get changed while I get dinner ready," said Susan.

"But I want to keep my uniform on. I'll be very careful and not spill anything on it."

"No, it's not for indoors. Now do what I said." The rising anger in her voice had the desired effect and Stanislav stomped off to his bedroom to change. Susan began preparing the small piece of beef which she had queued for over two hours to buy. It would be a suitable meal for one, not three. They might be filling children's heads with stories of socialist fairytales but the mothers in the long lines for the food shops with nearly empty shelves knew the unspoken truth. Like the Emperor in the folk tale, Gottwald's regime had no clothes but no one dare say so. Everything was in short supply apart from those things which weren't available at all unless you were a high ranking Party official.

Life in the Rubinstein household was considerably more comfortable. Food was in plentiful supply and the living space something the vast majority of Czechs could only dream about. Yet even the privileged had their problems.

Jakub listened to his father with disbelief. Autumn sunshine cascaded through the window, exposing not only dancing dust motes but more of the dark underbelly of this new world.

"How could you even contemplate doing such a thing to your own granddaughter?"

"Like I said, Jakub, there have been comments from within the Party. She's been seen out on the streets, she's been noticed."

"My God, you're no different to the Nazis."

"Take that back!" His father's face flamed like the fall leaves. "You of all people should know that is a bare faced lie. They murdered the disabled. We, on the other hand, look after them and place them in dedicated facilities with qualified staff who can give the best possible care."

"Hide them away in heartless institutions you mean so you can pretend all is perfect in your Communist dystopia while keeping contact with their families to an absolute minimum."

"Evinka will be placed in a home for afflicted children of Party members. She will have friends to play with, children like her, and appropriate schooling. If she stays here, she'll get none of that. I'll ensure you and your wife are able to make regular visits."

"Me and Ivetka want her here with us. Only we can give her the love she needs."

When Evinka had been born a few years earlier, they hadn't immediately noticed that she had down syndrome but it soon became apparent. Not that it made any difference to how her parents felt about her. She was the sweetest child imaginable and Jakub loved her with a passion.

"I've kept her in this house as long as I could. It's out of my hands," said Matous.

"Then we'll emigrate to the West."

"That's not possible." Matous' voice hardened. "She will be collected within the hour. I suggest you and Ivetka pack her things and reassure her, rather than unsettle her and upset the poor child."

Evinka wasn't reassured by the sight of the man and the woman who came, despite her parents' promises that she was going to a wonderful place and they would be coming to see her very soon. Her screams of fright and cries for help were hard even for Matous to bear. Sitting at his desk in his study, he put his hands over his ears.

Looking down from upstairs, Sara gripped the bannister tightly. She understood how traumatic it was to be taken away from family. She knew the damage it did to a child. Most would have thought Sara fortunate, she had been reunited with her family. But things had changed. Without her mother's example of love and gentleness, the family had become a remoter, more brittle thing. Radmila was a distant, disinterested stepmother, Yosef a fanatic for his cause, and her father's awful experiences at the hands of the Nazis had convinced him that the Communists' oppression was justified.

CHAPTER 38

Come November, Stanislav pleaded with his mother and grandfather to take him to a nation-wide commemoration. Teachers across the country had been directed to whip their classes into a frenzy to encourage maximum attendance. Many former celebrations had been replaced by those of socialist solidarity, such as International Women's Day, International Children's Day, and Liberation Day, which now centred around the myth that it was the Russians who had freed Prague rather than the citizens themselves. The star of them all, however, took place on 7 November, marking the 'Great Socialist Revolution' of 1917 in Russia. Adults joked amongst themselves that it was neither great, nor socialist, nor a revolution, but a coup by Lenin and a small band of followers, and that it had taken place in October.

Stanislav had already brought home a painting from school which he had done of the cruiser 'Aurora' from where the first shot had been fired to signal the assault on the Winter Palace in Saint Petersburg. He had also insisted his family listen while he recited the poem the schoolchildren had all been required to learn by heart, 'November 7th in Moscow'.

It was with reluctance that Stefan was pulled down the stairs by his grandson's eager hand.

"Hurry up or we'll be late."

Stefan sighed, he had seen what May Day had become. No longer a celebration of spring and love, the obedient masses instead paraded with huge portraits of their new gods: Lenin, Stalin and Gottwald.

To Stefan's surprise, this particular march was charming if one ignored what it was commemorating and chose instead to enjoy the spectacle. At the school gates the children each collected a paper lantern on a stick they had help make, their teacher first lighting the candle inside. The crowd marched through the darkened streets, the lanterns glowing like giant fireflies. It was pleasing to the eye and there was an absence of the shouting out of the usual manic Communist mantras.

On Kampa Island, Jakub wanted to move out of his father's but there was nowhere to go. Housing was in short supply and he and his wife didn't meet the criteria. Priority for the cramped apartments in the drab and poorly constructed blocks in the suburbs was given to those with children.

The Nazis had taken away Jakub's mother and

now the Communists had taken away his daughter. The man who had protected him from death in Terezin no longer existed. He had disappeared, kidnapped by ambition and the cult of Communism. Jakub chose revenge.

He worked in a lowly office job in the Ministry of Culture, one which had been bestowed upon him by his father. Nothing of much note ever crossed Jakub's desk. But his father brought government papers home to read, papers that might well have value to those on the sunny side of the Iron Curtain.

Jakub commenced a new night time routine. When he heard his father come up the stairs to bed, he would slip down to the man's study to begin reading and making notes.

In a narrow dead end street beneath the castle walls, the Thun Palace had been the British Embassy since Czechoslovakia had come into existence. Jakub walked up and down the street which led into it, hesitant to go any further. He might be seen. Courage ran away from him and he too left. He was wise to do so. Throughout the Cold War, the secret police watched who came and went from the embassy through a spy hole in a door opposite.

It was on the walk home that the idea came to him. He turned around and went back to Mala Strana and up the stairs to the apartment.

"Jakub. What are you doing here?"

In a hushed tone, he explained to Susan what had

happened to Evinka and what he wanted to do.

"You're British. I thought you would have a legitimate reason for going to the embassy."

"Well, actually you're right. I'm due to go and renew my passport soon but I really don't want to get involved. Paja as you know is in prison. I have our son to think of."

"You would have no involvement other than to make them aware of my offer and let me know where I should meet them if they are interested. That would be all."

"I don't know."

Jakub pressed his case. "Please. Think of your husband, what they've done to him, a war hero. Don't you want to do something for his sake? Isn't it something he would have done if only he was free to do so? He didn't let the Nazis stop him, and I doubt he would have let this despicable lot either."

"All right but what you ask is all I am going to do, nothing more."

It was in the shadows at the back of a cafe where cigarette smoke wafted upwards to create an indoor cloud that Jakub sat down next to a table occupied by a man of unremarkable appearance. Without looking at Jakub, the man beckoned with his hand from under the table. Jakub reached inside his coat pocket for his notes and placed them into the man's outstretched palm who deftly transferred them to his own pocket. Not once glancing in Jakub's direction, the man told him the place and time for the next hand-over. He downed his coffee in one wincing as if he had sucked on a lemon- ersatz Soviet coffee was a poor imitation of the real thing that they served in the embassy - and departed. When Jakub stepped outside several minutes later to be blinded by the low winter sunshine, he nonetheless smiled, the first time he had done so in several weeks. At last, he was getting his own back.

His sister, Sara, walked home with poise and elegance in a city where both were in short supply from a people burdened by the weight of drab uniformity. Communist fashions were dull, utility over beauty, function over style, flat shoes over heels, headscarves over hats. Glamour had died.

The city herself had become haggard, her clothing shabby and torn. Save for the bight colours of Communist propaganda posters which portrayed enthusiastic workers striding towards imaginary sunlit uplands, black and grey were the colours of Prague. War damage remained largely untouched and maintenance ignored. Most buildings hadn't felt the refreshing lick of a paintbrush since the 1930s.

Instead, the city had been rebranded. The square in front of the Rudolfinum, known as Smetana Square during the years of freedom, and renamed Mozartplatz during the Nazi occupation, was now Red Army Square with a huge five-pointed star inlaid in the ground.

Sara took little notice as she passed by. Yellow stars or red stars were things she didn't want to think about. She was young and a favoured one. Not only because of her father's position but also because of her ability to leap and twist and fly through the air with grace. She had become an accomplished gymnast.

"Guess what, Jakub," Sara beamed as she came through the front door.

"What?"

"I've been picked for the Olympic team."

"That's nice," said her brother in a monotone voice. Sara didn't reprimand him for his under-whelming congratulation as once she would have. She knew the light had gone out in his life since they took Evinka away. Sara hated that too, but what could she do? Nothing. What point would there be refusing her place in protest? Absolutely none. There were plenty who would be eager to take her spot. And she wouldn't get to see Edvard again if she did. A fellow gymnast, he had a mop of unruly hair and a moustache and the body of a Greek god. His invitation to take a coffee together after the training session had been a surprise. Sara had thought the infatuation was only one way.

"I hear a rumour that congratulations might be in order," he said with a toothy grin. Sara nodded. "Well done. Me too, I've been picked as well. It's so exciting to think we are going to Helsinki. I've never been abroad."

"Me neither."

"Oh, I thought given who your father is that maybe you took foreign vacations."

"No such luck. He's wedded to his work and interested in little else. What about your family?"

"We're an ordinary bunch. Part of the masses as they say, though I suppose I shouldn't get political with a government minister's daughter."

"You'd be wrong to make assumptions. I'm not like my father."

"I'm glad to hear it. Are you free Sunday?"

"I can be." Sara teased with her espresso eyes.

Matous' own congratulations for his daughter's achievement irked her. The worth of anything to him was judged by its contribution to his beloved cause.

"I am very pleased. By succeeding for our country you will be showing the world the benefits of the socialist system, how we nurture talent and produce athletes of world beating quality."

Sara made no comment. Her father was an annoying buzzing in her ears these days. It wasn't worth wasting the energy of her emotions in worrying about what he thought. Her sport was what she cared about, the adrenaline fuelled high that gymnastics gave her. When she somersaulted or backflipped through the air, she was free as a bird. The terror of her childhood, that constant worry of being found and of never seeing her parents again could be locked in a cupboard at the back of her mind. Her early years hadn't been a source of security on which to build a solid foundation for an adult life. Gymnastics was her way of coping with the past, it was her drug.

When her coach offered her tablets to enhance her performance, she didn't hesitate to take them.

CHAPTER 39

For the masses there was Spartakiad. Stanislav persuaded his grandfather to accompany him and his mother to the Strahov stadium to witness the spectacle. Located beyond Petrin hill, the stadium was gargantuan. It was the world's largest, three times longer and three times wider than a conventional football stadium, accommodating two hundred thousand spectators.

To celebrate 'liberation', countless thousands of Czech gymnasts poured into the arena to perform synchronised movements, each part of a human murmuration. Czech folk music which had met with the censor's approval blared from the speakers around the grounds.

"Wasn't that great?" said Stanislav, his cheeks flushed pink with excitement as they filed out of the stadium after the performance to join the departing crowds spreading out from the venue and filling the surrounding neighbourhoods.

"Did you ever hear of Sokol, Stanicek?" asked his grandfather.

"No."

"Well, that is what they have copied, or I should

say hijacked. It was a wonderful thing, started last century to build national consciousness and a healthy, caring nation. I used to take part myself when I wasn't much older than you. It also required us to be ethical and to put the education and prosperity of our families first and to help our communities."

"Like Communism then."

"No, it was freer, and spontaneous. It came from the bottom up, it wasn't organised and manipulated from above."

Stanislav wrinkled his nose and furrowed his eyebrows, "I don't understand the difference."

Stefan didn't respond. How could he or anyone get today's youth to understand the ideals of freedom and justice which both he and his son's generation had fought for when, like tank treads, the education system was crushing that history and paving it over with a new warped and self serving narrative.

Even as late as 1947, close to one in ten Czechs had been involved in Sokol. Meaning falcon, a bird which is swift and intelligent so it can survive in a world of more powerful birds of prey, exactly as Czechoslovakia had tried to find a way of surviving in a world of larger, more powerful nations. Now the Sokol movement had been buried, considered reactionary. Spartakiad was its cult like caricature sanctioned by the Communist regime.

When they got home, Stefan retreated to his

workshop. In the make believe world of puppets, he could pretend that the Communist regime was also not real, only a bad dystopian novel. Absent-mindedly he flicked the switch on the radio hoping for some soothing music to carve to. But yet again an overbearing voice was condemning the activities of 'counter revolutionaries'. Stefan sighed and leaned forward to turn the radio off but stopped. Dagmar Danekova. The name seized his attention. She and others had, so the announcer claimed, confessed to passing secrets to the enemies of the State to undermine the People's revolution. There would be a People's trial. Everything these days was prefaced by 'the People' as if it was they who decided what was allowed and what was not, instead of the small clique in power which claimed well over ninety per cent of the population had voted for them when there was only one political party to choose from in their sham elections.

A shiver caught the nape of Stefan's neck and made him wriggle his shoulders. Was Dagmar, who like his son, had managed to survive the Nazis, destined to follow in Pavel's footsteps or worse?

Stefan thought about visiting Matous and asking him to intervene. Yet he couldn't bring himself to do so, his pride told him not to go. He refused to seek favours any longer from his one time friend. And, after all, what good would it do? Was saving her from execution only to spend years in a la-

bour camp really helping her? His son was probably wishing that he had been hung rather than
live the life he had to endure.

On Kampa Island, Jakub impatiently waited for
night to arrive. Today he and his wife had been
allowed to visit their daughter for the first time.
The bars at the windows and the random shouting from behind closed doors along with the
stench of urine as they walked down the long
corridor did nothing to reassure them. Evinka
had run into their arms and refused to let go
when she had been brought to them by one of the
unsmiling staff members.

"Fifteen minutes only," pronounced the woman.

"What have I done wrong? Take me home, please
take me home." Evinka's pleas were unbearable.
Jakub hated that he couldn't protect his daughter. What kind of an excuse for a man was
he? What if their new child his wife was about
to give birth to didn't meet the State's require-
ments, would he stand by and let another child
of his be taken away?

This time at home he got down on his knees and
begged his father. "I need to get her out of there
and back here with us."

His father extended his arm and pulled him up.
His son's behaviour made him uncomfortable.

"She wouldn't ever be able to go outside."

"We don't care. Love is more important than
fresh air."

"All right, I'll see what I can do but give me a while. I need to time it right. There are rumours of a purge in the Party."

"A purge?"

"There's infighting between two factions. It depends who comes out on top."

"Which faction are you in?"

"I'm trying to avoid choosing for as long as I can. If I make the wrong choice, it could be fatal."

In the depths of the night, Jakub crept into his father's study. Even if they got Evinka back, he didn't intend stopping. He would continue to do all he could to weaken this hateful regime. Only if it collapsed would his daughter be free to have the childhood which she deserved.

Entering the study, he shut the door before switching on the light. He took a sharp intake of breath. Jakub hadn't expected to see the person who was already there waiting for him.

CHAPTER 40

"Yosef, what are you doing here?" Jakub's voice croaked. He hardly ever saw his brother these days. After his promotion, Yosef had been given a comfortable apartment in the New Town and rarely came to his father's home.

"I think the more pertinent question is what are you doing here, and in the middle of the night?" His brothers eyes burned through his circular glasses like a magnifying glass concentrating the sun's light onto paper.

"I couldn't sleep. I came down to read a book so I wouldn't disturb Ivetka."

"Really? I don't ever recall seeing you read a book the whole time I've known you. Tell me, why are you passing secrets to the British?"

"What?" Those penetrating eyes of his brother were making Jakub sweat. "You must be mistaken, I have no idea what you're talking about."

"Don't lie, brother. Take a look at this." Yosef reached inside his suit pocket and handed Jakub a photograph. "That man you're talking to works at the British embassy."

"I...I don't know him," stuttered Jakub. "He was

merely asking for directions."

"Enough of the lying, we have others." Yosef spoke in a measured way but there was gravel in his tone. "Why, Jakub? Why betray your own father? You were always the favoured one. When we were growing up, whatever I did was never enough. But you, whatever you did or didn't do was fine by him."

"He took my daughter away. I don't expect you'd understand not having a child of your own. I hate your bloody system, treating children like this, it's inhuman."

"So I'm just supposed to ignore what you did and pretend it didn't happen? No, Jakub, what you've done is unforgivable, it's treason. You can face torture and execution if you want and bring your family down with you or do the decent thing." Yosef removed the gun which was hidden by his jacket from the holster on his trouser belt and offered it to his brother whose expression was one of disbelief. "What's it to be, Jakub?"

Yosef had already slipped out of the house when his father came downstairs in response to the shot. Ivetka and Sara held each other as they waited at the top of the staircase. The shock sent Ivetka into labour. After the funeral, she asked her father-in-law to arrange an apartment in the suburbs for her and her baby son and he agreed to do so.

Stefan wondered if the world had gone mad

when he heard reports on the radio of meetings all over Prague where citizens were baying for the death penalty for the 'traitors' on trial. The regime had deliberately wound up the masses, baiting them as if throwing a piece of raw meat at a pack of wolves. The trials were broadcast live, the defendants each confirming the veracity of their confessions. Stefan didn't believe them for one moment. He had known Dagmar well enough to recognise that it was all a fabrication. They must have been tortured to say what they did, nothing else could explain it.

As the sentences were pronounced, Stefan sat still as a statue, listening intently. Death, life imprisonment, death, death. When Dagmar received life imprisonment, it didn't make him feel relief that she wasn't to be hung. She was innocent like the rest. Denied justice and guilty only of one thing, wanting a free country.

When Stanislav came home one day in tears, Stefan saw an opportunity.

"What's wrong?" asked Susan.

"Tatka. I hate him."

"Your father? Why?"

"The others told me he's a spy, an enemy of the People. That I'm the son of a class enemy and should be thrown out of the Pioneers."

Stefan had heard enough. "Listen to me, Stanicek. They're lying, lying because they've been lied to exactly as you have. Your father is a true patriot and a hero. Sit down and let me tell you all about your father." Stefan recounted his son's past as Stanislav listened, eyes wide with attention. "So don't believe them and don't be fooled. He's a fine man, a father to be proud of."

Stefan choked with emotion and his grandson threw his arms around him to comfort him.

"I'm finished with the Pioneers, I never want to go again."

Stefan smiled and tussled the boy's hair. He had his grandson back. Someone who maybe one day when he was grown would continue the family legacy and fight for freedom.

Sara had been devastated by her brother's suicide and almost lost her place on the Olympic team as a result. That he would kill himself didn't make any sense. Yes, he was probably depressed by Evinka having been taken away, but he had a new child coming and a wife he adored and who loved him back. Her father didn't want to talk about it and Ivetka had moved out. Sara therefore decided to visit Yosef, something which she had never done before.

It was with some trepidation that she stepped down from the tram and walked the few steps to his building. She almost didn't enter. Yosef was so much older than her and they had never been close. Sara had been only a little girl when he had left Prague to go to war. When he returned, he had become someone she found intimidating. There was a coldness to him as if those Russian winters had chilled his very soul.

The old lift had the appearance of an animal's cage at the zoo, it and the lift shaft surrounded by the staircase. She got in and pressed the button and it juddered upwards. Reaching the top floor, she knocked on his door. There was no answer. She tried the handle. The door wasn't locked and she entered.

"Is that you, Yosef?"

A blonde haired young man emerged from the bedroom. His look was one of guilt as if he'd been caught stealing. Unshaven, he was wearing a silk dressing gown and probably nothing else, thought Sara.

"Hello, I'm Sara, his sister. Could I wait until Yosef gets back?"

"I… I suppose so. I'll go get dressed. Yosef let's me use his shower, mine's broken."

Sara surveyed her brother's domain. The furniture looked as if it had been here since the days of the Austro-Hungarian Empire. Unlike her brother's orderly personality, his home was untidy. Plates from breakfast or more probably last night's dinner, given that wine glasses and an empty wine bottle remained on the dark mahogany dining table. Two plates and two wine glasses.

Sara wandered to the window. Overlooking the trees of Slovansky island and the Vltava, her brother enjoyed a fine view up here in his secret, unseen world.

"Sara, how did you get in?" Yosef's voice betrayed an uncharacteristic nervousness.

"Your friend let me in."

"Oh yes, Max. He's staying for a couple of days in between moving apartments."

Max appeared from a bedroom. "You're back. I was telling Sara how you let me in to use the shower. I'll be off now."

Sara looked at her brother and raised her eyebrows in a silent question. Never before had she wielded any power over him. She had always been irrelevant to him.

"You won't tell anyone will you?" said Yosef after his friend had left.

"Why would I? Although I'd like to know what you know about our brother."

"I don't know anything. He must have been mentally disturbed."

Sara persisted. "I don't believe you. You have files on everybody, I want the truth. Be honest with me and you can rest assured that your secret's safe with me."

"He was spying, for the British."

"Spying? Why?"

"To get back at father for taking Evinka away."

Sara sat down in one of the Louis XIV style chairs. Deep in contemplation, she stroked her lips moving her index finger back and forth across them. Suddenly she dropped her hand. "Were you... were you there that night?" Her brother didn't answer. Anger infused her cheeks like a ripe peach. "Oh my god, it was you. You gave him the gun to shoot himself. How could you, your own brother?" Sara was already standing.

"I offered him a way out. A trial would have ruined all of us, and he still would have died."

Tears streaming down her face, Sara ran from the apartment and didn't stop until she was outside in the street where she gulped air as she fought nausea. Shaken by what she had discovered, Sara sat on a bench by the river for a long while peering into the waters below. She had spent too much of her life almost drowning in despair. Each time things seemed to be turning a corner, another wave would hit her and she would go under again. Maybe she should stop resisting what seemed to be her fate, jump in the Vlatva and accept the peace that would surely come, a welcome end to the constant anxiety that gnawed at her soul and sapped her will to live. Sara had no one left to turn to, only Edvard, but she couldn't burden him with her past. That would scare him off.

She stood up and glanced around furtively. There were few people about and none who looked like they would jump in after her. She walked to the edge and looked down at her reflection which appeared to be calling her.

Now, do it, just do it, she scolded herself.

Her feet stuck to the paving. She couldn't. This was madness. There was still hope. There was Edvard.

Later that day, the couple met on the rocky promontory above the river where once had stood Vysehrad, or high castle, the place where according to Czech legend Libuse, a chieftain's daughter, founded the city to be named 'Praha', meaning ford or rapid. Only some ramparts remained. The young couple wandered through the park there and into the cemetery where the composers Dvorak and Smetana, and Alfons Mucha, the famous art nouveau artist, along with many other notables of Czech culture lie buried.

"Coming here reminds me of what our nation achieved and could do again, wonderful music, art and literature," said Edvard.

"If we were free to do so."

"Do you mean that?"

"Absolutely, I'm tired of pretending, pretending that all is wonderful in our socialist paradise. Does that shock you?"

"No, it pleases me. I feel the same way. I've been thinking about getting out, but I've been torn as I'd miss you too much."

"And me you." She leaned towards him, encouraging his kiss. "I'd come with you if you could find a way."

"Helsinki. It's our chance to defect. But what about your family?"

"I don't have one any more, not now Jakub's gone."

CHAPTER 41

The Czechoslovak athletes were barracked in cramped quarters with other Eastern bloc competitors to avoid them being 'corrupted' by western influence. The Helsinki Olympics was the first time the Soviet Union had participated in such a sporting event with the West. Their decision to do so was driven by the goal of wanting to win the most medals to demonstrate the superiority of Communism.

"What's the plan?" whispered Sara as they passed in the canteen.

"I don't know," said Edvard. "I hadn't thought we would be kept segregated from the other athletes under lock and key and constant supervision. Maybe in the gymnastics hall we'll get a chance to slip away."

When the team bus dropped them there, their minders herded them inside, keeping them confined to their single sex changing rooms until the moment of performance.

Sara never got to see Edvard. Tense and distracted, she stumbled on a couple of her landings.

Her coach berated Sara through gritted teeth when she came off the mat. "What's wrong with you! You've probably just cost us the silver medal for the team event."

"I'm sorry."

"Sorry's not good enough. If we only get the bronze, it will be your fault."

Sara sat on the end of the bench with bated breath as the scores for her team were announced. The Soviet Union took the gold, Hungary the silver and Czechoslovakia the bronze. It was a victory for Communism but the coach didn't see it that way.

"Losing to Hungary is a humiliation, your gymnastics career is over." Czechs had not forgotten that Hungary had seized some of their country as part of the German occupation. More than ever now Sara wanted to defect, but an opportunity to do so was proving elusive.

Passing in the accommodation block with no one else in sight, Edvard imparted his plan.

"The closing ceremony is our only chance. You need to stay as close to me as you can."

As they marched into the stadium, Edvard squeezed her hand. "I'm hoping that when we're all assembled, there'll be so many of us that we can get out unnoticed with another team."

Like Roman Legions each nation paraded behind their flag, assembling in the central area inside the athletics track. When the President of the International Olympic Committee finished his speech and declared the Games closed, the American athletes broke into spontaneous cheering, bouncing around and hugging each other. America had won but not by much, beating the Soviet Union by only five medals. Other athletes joined in the celebration and the neat lines and divisions melted like ice cream.

Sara felt her hand grabbed by Edvard and she was pulled sideways. Without a word, he pushed through the chaos, never once looking back.

"Help, please. We want to escape Communists," Edvard asked of a group of athletes in faltering English.

"Hey, what do you think you're doing?" Two of the minders who had been amongst the Czechoslovak athletes were tugging at Sara and Edvard by the arm. Luckily, burly American athletes surrounded them, insisting they let go. Outnumbered they did so, scowling with an anger that would have been tinged with fear.

"Your family will pay for this," one of them called out to Edvard. Back in Prague these men would be disciplined for failing to stop the escape and probably be thrown out of the secret police.

"Come," said one of the Americans who led the couple out of the stadium. Soon they were in a car en route to the American embassy.

"What about your family, Edvard? You heard what that man said." asked Sara.

"My parents knew what I was going to do, I told them. They encouraged me, said not to worry about them. Maybe if you contact your father he'll help."

"I doubt it. Are you sure you still want to do this?"

"Definitely."

At the embassy, they were debriefed separately and within hours they were on a plane to a US military base in Germany on their way to the United States.

Before the day was out, Matous had been summoned to President Gottwald's office in Prague castle. In the back of the official car as it sped up the hill, Matous wondered what was going to happen. The purge had probably begun. He was as confident as he could be that he wouldn't be implicated. He had been most careful to avoid any controversy.

One of the large double doors to Gottwald's office was opened for Matous and shut firmly behind him.

"To what do I owe this honour, President?" Matous began perspiring, Gottwald's expression was one of ill concealed fury.

"Sit," ordered Gottwald. The man rose from behind his desk and wandered back and forth behind Matous as if a lion eyeing an injured gazelle. "Your daughter has defected."

It was a well aimed verbal punch taking Matous by complete surprise. "Surely someone must be mistaken, she and her team won bronze. She loves her sport, it's her life."

"Her sport maybe but not her country. She and that boyfriend of hers have brought shame on us all, handed the Americans a massive propaganda victory, and after the socialist states did so well."

"Do you know how I can contact her? Maybe I can-"

"It's too late for that. You are to mention her defection to no one."

"Of course." Matous suppressed the sense of loss that was tearing at his insides. First his son and now his daughter. The only child left in Prague wasn't even his own.

Gottwald ceased pacing and came to stand directly in front of him, hands behind his back. "Your family has become a liability, a suicide and now a defection. It has also made you a liability to the Party."

"Please, no one need ever know," pleaded Matous. The Party was his work, his purpose, his life.

"The public will never be told of your daughter's betrayal but the Party knows and cannot be compromised. You will be moved tomorrow to a worker's apartment in the suburbs. I have a letter of resignation for you to sign." Matous couldn't conceal his feelings of devastation. "Don't look so crestfallen, Comrade, you may find that you've had a lucky escape."

The bleak man-made forest of the high rises became Matous' land of exile. From the tenth floor he looked out over concrete and harsh right angles. His beautiful Prague of decadent Gothic, Baroque, Art Nouveau and Cubism didn't extend this far. This new world was one of utilitarian and brutalist architecture.

Fifty-six and his career at an end, his new job was as a gardner in Letna Park. Radmila would resent her changed life, denied the privileges and luxuries that had been afforded to a government minister and his wife. Yet she too could do nothing about it, she would never be given her own place to live if she left him. An impoverished, joyless existence stretched out before them both.

Later that year, Rudolf Slanksy, second in command after Gottwald, and thirteen other high ranking officials, ten of whom were Jewish, were charged with a 'Zionist imperialist conspiracy' to overthrow the government. Listening on the radio, Stefan waited for Matous' name to be read out as one of the accused. He had played with fire and would get burned. Stefan would never mention it to anyone but he experienced something close to disappointment when Matous' name wasn't among them. Predictably, all of the accused were found guilty and most were executed.

CHAPTER 42

Stalin's death in early 1953, followed only a week later by the death of Czechoslovakia's President, Gottwald, sent whispered hopes across the city like an early morning mist beginning to lift and promising sunshine to come. Life might now change for the better, but the opposite proved to be true.

"You won't believe what the bastards have just announced," Stefan ranted to Susan, spitting out crumbs of bread across the dining table as he spoke. "They're robbing us of our money."

"Taking your money? How can that be?"

"A so called currency reform. Old money to be swopped for new, savings in the ratio fifty for one. All my life I've been careful and saved. Now most of it will be confiscated. I pray to God the people will finally rise up."

Later, in his workshop, Stefan took his axe to his puppets of Gottwald and Stalin, attacking them with venom and wishing that the real men were still alive and could face justice for the misery they had inflicted on his family and his country. He didn't stop until they were unrecognisable.

Stefan didn't want to be reminded of the tyrants. The people never rose up, the apparatus of State control was too strong and the chains of oppression too tight.

The next day, Susan suggested the family take a stroll and visit Letna Park to take her father-in-law's mind off his worries. Elevated on the northern bank of the Vltava as it turns eastwards, it offers fine views over the Old Town. Walking its leafy paths in dappled late spring sunshine, it did raise Stefan's spirits reminding him of when he and Marta had brought their children here when they were young, halcyon days of laughter and bright, innocent smiles. Raised his spirits until he saw the gigantic monstrosity under construction. Already the figure of Stalin was recognisable, a European Genghis Khan. At over fifteen metres, the monument would be Europe's largest. A monolith to shout out the city's subservience. When completed, statues of revolutionary workers would be lined up behind him. The locals would mock it, calling it 'the bread line' or 'the meat queue'.

Stefan's outing had been spoiled. "I'm going back but you and Stanicek should stay and enjoy yourselves"

"Are you feeling unwell?" asked Susan.

"No, just a little tired. I slept badly last night."

Stefan felt like crying but he had shed so many tears over recent years, he didn't think he could have any left. His wife dead, his daughter gone forever, his son maybe never coming home, and now his retirement savings gone. How could his life once so full of promise have become locked in a past of memories because the present was so hard to endure.

He walked on, passing one of the gardeners, trowel in hand and a cap on his head. The man had a hand on his lower back as he stretched his torso upwards as if he ached. Stefan came to a sudden halt and turned. "Matous?"

The man approached him, pushing his cap back and leaving some soil on his forehead in the process. "Ah, Stefan. See how the mighty are fallen. It must please you."

"Nothing pleases me under this regime, but maybe now you understand what it's like for the rest of us."

"I must admit that sometimes I struggle with my beliefs. Like religion there are times when you question it, but we are striving for a better world however imperfectly. I was unlucky, circumstance made me an embarrassment to the Party. Jakub killed himself and Sara defected."

"I'm very sorry to hear about Jakub, very sorry. But I'm happy for Sara. After the childhood she endured, she deserves to be free. Where is she?"

"In America, but she never writes. How is Paja?"

"He is only permitted to send us a postcard twice a year. He tells us everything is fine but I know he's only saying that for our benefit. I can't forget what you let happen, nor forgive."

Stefan didn't say goodbye and continued on his way. The past would be his future, how could it be otherwise? Just because Matous had fallen on hard times altered nothing. He still clung to the fantasy of Communism and a belief that the ends justified the means.

Contrary to what he had expected to be the case, Matous found himself enjoying his new position. Tending flowers and watching them grow and then bloom, enjoying the rain rather than seeking to avoid it, and being a part of the changing seasons rather than someone who barely noticed them through his office window, was a good tonic for all that had happened to him. And no longer did he have sleepless nights about whether he might be arrested for being identified with the wrong faction of the Party. There was a peace in his life which he had rarely experienced.

Matous bought himself a secondhand violin and played for the first time since he had been a prisoner in Terezin. Radmila and he found fulfilment playing together in the evenings. Never again would they play in a grand concert hall but that no longer mattered. It made their drab apartment fade away, and lifted them into a world of symphonic beauty. The melancholy of certain pieces helped him grieve for all he had lost, the jauntiness of others made him smile.

Matous decided to visit his dead son's wife, Ivetka. He found her sitting on a bench in the children's playground near to the concrete tower where she lived.

"Do you mind if I join you?"

She didn't answer him. Getting up, she called out to a young boy who had just come down the slide. "Time to go home, Mirek."

"Please, Ivetka-"

"Leave us alone." Her eyes were aflame with loathing. "We want nothing to do with you. You let them take my daughter away, and my husband killed himself because of it."

Matous could only watch as his grandson came running to his mother. The resemblance to Jakub was both striking and heartbreaking. The boy stared at the man.

"Who is that?" he asked his mother

"No one. Let's go."

CHAPTER 43

It was two years later that Stefan opened the door to a person whom he hardly recognised. This man hadn't enjoyed the good fortune to only be condemned to gardening. Not one wisp of hair remained on his head, his face was gaunt, several of his teeth had fallen out and his eyes were no longer vibrant. Instead, they seemed to be those of a much older man and one who was tired of life.

"They let me out."

Stefan embraced his son. Susan shrieked with delight and ran across the room to join them. Stanislav stood back, too shocked by his father's spectral appearance to come over.

Pavel went towards him. "Hello, Stanicek. My, how you've grown, you're as tall as me and almost a man. I'm so proud of you." That overwhelmed his son who burst into tears and flung his arms around his father.

When Susan cuddled up to her husband that night his ribcage was sharp and his libido gone.

"Sorry, I'm so tired."

"You have nothing to apologise for. I'm just so

happy you are back. Don't you worry, we'll get you fighting fit again."

Yet Pavel coughed and wheezed like a man three times his age. When his wife saw blood on his pillow, she insisted that he see the doctor who referred him to the hospital.

After Susan and Stanislav had gone to bed on the day of the diagnosis, Stefan sat down in the armchair next to where his son was seated and stretched out his arm, laying his hand on Pavel's. "Susan's told me."

"I've failed my family. I should never have tried to flee. None of this would have happened. Stanicek would have had a father all these years, and Susan a husband and not forced to work cleaning the streets."

"You mustn't think like that, son. None of this is your fault, it's the fault of the pigs who rule us, who lie and condemn people for wanting a good life for their families. You must enjoy your time with yours, not waste it blaming yourself. You're a hero and always will be. The failures and the cowards, those are people like Matous and his son, Yosef, who put their own advancement before the lives of others."

They sat in contemplative silence in the way that men can, neither needing to talk. Pavel didn't want to speak about what he had gone through but there was one thing he was keen to tell his father.

"Not long after I got there, I met someone who

knew you. In fact, he saved my life. We were trapped in the mine by a rockfall. I was ready to give up but he wouldn't let me, and I'm grateful he didn't or I never would have seen you all again. He said his name was Rudi, that you'd saved his life and he wanted to repay you."

"Rudi," Stefan uttered the word in quiet surprise. "That's a name I never thought I'd hear again. Is he still in the camp?"

"No, he was being held as a prisoner of war and was about to be released and sent to Germany. He said he was caught trying to leave the country as a civilian with others being deported but someone recognised him as having been in the Wehrmacht."

That night Stefan was awake until almost dawn, thinking not only of his son but of his own youth. Remembering the three friends, like brothers, looking out for each other. Living a simple life but such a good one, not knowing what lay beyond their teenage horizon and assuming life would always be as uncomplicated and blissful as it then was.

Stefan used to think of Rudi as the one who had joined the enemy. And indeed he had, but Rudi hadn't let that lead him to betray Stefan. Rudi could have arrested Stefan when he found Dagmar in his apartment but Rudi had chosen not to. As far as Stefan was concerned, Matous too had joined an enemy. Stefan would never understand why after the terrible suffering he and his family had experienced at the hands of the Nazis, Matous could have been such a strong advocate for dictatorship. And unlike Rudi, Matous had chosen to betray Stefan and his family, refusing to call out Yosef as a liar, and now Stefan's son was going to die because of that.

Pavel's death a few months later from cancer caused by radiation drove Stefan to thoughts of suicide, but needing to be there for his grandson stopped him taking his own life. He had been a substitute father for the boy. Stanislav had lost his own father, he didn't need more hurt to cope with.

Stefan was old enough to retire but he didn't. Not only had the government plundered his life savings and the state pension small but time was one thing which he didn't desire. An emptiness that would only fill with sorrow so he continued making puppets. His creations were works of art, not the mass produced ones churned out of the factories these days to be sold in the West to attract sorely needed capitalist currency for the government.

Puppets were his only friends. He talked to them and in his head they talked back. They chatted about the good old days. Together they concocted fanciful plots to free Prague from their wicked masters.

Stefan developed a new show, an allegory for what they were living through. It was his way of hitting back and reminding people of how they were being duped. Children loved it for its classic tale of good versus evil. The adults accompanying them loved its subversiveness and clapped loudly with approval at the thinly disguised attack on their government.

"I have devised a wonderful new system of governance," the puppet king would say to his wife.

"And what might that be?" asked his queen.

"I will make everybody equal."

"But how can you possibly do that? We don't have enough money to improve the lot of the poor, there are too many of them."

"I know. I will make everyone equally poor."

"But then you will have no tax revenue to pay for our lifestyle or for a war to divert the people's attention when they get restless."

"I've already thought of that. I will confiscate everyone's property and savings and pay them only a pittance for their work."

"But surely the people will rebel."

"That's why the police and the officers in the army will be paid well and have special privileges to keep them loyal."

It was under a dismal sky when Stefan was trudging through the wet slush of a late winter's day, slush that was speckled black from the particles of pollution drifting in relentlessly from factories farther out, that a woman crossed his path. When she smiled and said his name, it took him a few moments to register. Her hair, strands of which peeped out from under her navy blue headscarf, was almost as white as snow used to be and her face had become somewhat wrinkled. "Dagmar? I thought you'd got life."

"I did but when they became less Stalinist they relented and released me. They probably decided that a pensioner was no longer a threat to national security. Sadly those they hung, such as Milada Horakova, can't be brought back."

"Yes it was a monstrous thing they did, but I'm glad you've been freed."

"Well, goodbye, Stefan. It was nice to see you."

He thought he detected a wistful look in her eyes. "Wait. We should meet up, for old time's sake."

This time she didn't refuse. "All right. I'd offer to cook you dinner but all I have is a bedroom. The kitchen is shared with four others."

"Then let me take you out for dinner."

"Only if you let me pay for myself."

"If you insist. Still as independent as ever I see."

Restaurant was too grand a description for an establishment with poor quality food and lack of choice, but candlelight did create an ambience in the underground cellar with ancient stone walls and curved ceilings where diners talked quietly not knowing who might be listening to their conversations.

"You must be shocked to see the old woman I have become," said Dagmar in response to Stefan's rather intense gaze. "My hair changed colour almost overnight when they arrested me. It must have been the stress."

"I don't see age. In those eyes I still see a young woman, a woman who cared and sacrificed herself to try and make this world a better place. The beauty that comes from being a good person never fades."

Dagmar laughed. "That's probably because you're not wearing glasses. But I'll accept the compliment, I rarely get one. In fact, I can't remember the last time I did."

The couple started seeing each other regularly. Dagmar had mellowed, or perhaps more correctly her ambition to make a difference had been squashed by the boots of totalitarianism. When Stefan asked Susan what she thought of his plans, she was delighted.

"That's wonderful news. Of course I approve, you deserve to be happy."

Stanislav agreed to be best man, and under the unwelcome portraits of President Novotny and Russia's Khrushchev in the palace of weddings Stefan finally married the person he had fallen in love with almost a lifetime ago.

Now eighteen, Stanislav had to join the Czechoslovak People's Army for his two years military service so Susan decided to return to England for an extended visit.

Stefan who had once dreaded the prospect of his grandson leaving home found that his life had unexpectedly been transformed. He and Dagmar had found a comfortable love, not one of passion but one of companionship and support. A love the State didn't control and couldn't take away.

CHAPTER 44

After his release from the army, Stanislav married his pregnant girlfriend.

"It was the other way round in my day," commented his grandfather on hearing the news.

"Well, things have changed. Having a baby is the only way for young people to get their own apartment," replied Dagmar.

The young couple moved out to the characterless suburbs, and after a brief trip back to visit her new grandson, Susan returned to England where she too had met someone she was to marry. She had come weighed down with consumer goods that were unobtainable in Czechoslovakia.

"How on earth did you get all of this through Customs?" Stefan had asked when the family gathered in Stanislav's new apartment.

"By bribing the Customs officer."

"Ah yes, that's the way everything works here. We are all equal but those with money can get whatever they want."

Stanislav's wife went to answer the door and brought in their neighbour.

"This is Ivetka, she and her son live next door.

She's brought us some tomatoes. There were some available this morning."

"I know you, Ivetka," said Stefan smiling as he rose from his chair. "You are Matous' daughter-in-law. I was sorry to hear about your husband."

"It's ten years now. Time is a great healer but thank you."

"How is Matous?" Stefan asked out of politeness rather than genuine interest.

"I couldn't tell you, we don't speak. He had Evinka, who you may remember, sent away."

"Evinka, of course I remember her."

"She's almost an adult now and will spend her life in an institution. I am only permitted to see her twice a year. Anyway, I mustn't interrupt your family gathering. Nice to see you again."

Travelling home in the tram, Dagmar touched Stefan's arm to attract his attention.

"I wonder if Matous regrets what he did. You have a grandson who adores you, he one who he never sees."

"The last time I saw him he was still a communist despite all that happened to him."

"And Rudi, I suppose we'll never know what finally happened to him."

"I imagine he was reunited with his family when he got sent back to Germany."

"Do you forgive him?"

"Of course, he saved Paja in the mine which allowed him to see his family again. And he let both of us go free when he should have arrested us."

"Maybe you should think about forgiving Matous. We all make mistakes, think of the hurt we must have caused Marta."

Stefan moved his arm away from his wife's touch. The anger still within him came to the surface. "After what he did, and what happened to you too? How can you say such a thing?"

"I know it's a dilemma. However, he didn't personally order the arrest of Paja or my arrest for that matter. I would have still been imprisoned whether or not Matous was in the government, and Paja would have been executed without his intervention."

"Execution would have been a blessing compared to what he went through. Years in a hell on earth only to die a painful death from what they did to him. I was unfaithful to my wife but I didn't end her life. Matous could have saved Paja but he chose not to."

Stefan turned his head away and looked out of the window for the rest of the ride home.

When the sound of an explosion reverberated around the city one autumn morning in 1962 Stefan set out to investigate, Dagmar's pleas to be careful ringing in his ear. Overhearing conversations that indicated the blast had come from Letna, he headed in that direction. Police blocked the way of those hoping to take a closer look. A large cloud of dust was still settling. Yet even from a distance the security services couldn't hide the fact that Stalin's monument was being obliterated. It took several days and eight hundred kilograms of explosives to blow it up entirely, leaving only the plinth on which it stood and a mountain of rubble which was to lie there for weeks.

"Well?" asked Dagmar when Stefan returned.

"It's Stalin's monument, they're blowing it up."

"About time. Khrushchev denounced him years ago. The government must have decided it was an embarrassment but it's not going to change people's lives."

And it didn't. Any hope that it was a sign of liberalisation proved to be misplaced. Stefan and most inhabitants stopped thinking about change. The Nazis had occupied the city for six years, the Communists it seemed would last for as long as the Hapsburgs.

Reaching his seventies, Stefan accepted that his beautiful city would not be free again in his lifetime. The winter of his life was fast approaching and his dreams wouldn't be realised.

In the depths of Prague's own winter of 1968, with Moscow's blessing unpopular leader Novotny was replaced by Alexander Dubcek. Like robots, in the Old Town Square, soldiers and loyal Party members stood in closely packed and regimented lines, filling the enormous space to celebrate twenty years since the Communist coup. Never had the dictatorship looked more enduring.

Then the unexpected happened. Watching their grainy black and white television, Stefan and Dagmar intuitively reached for each other's hand as they watched the evening news report with smiles on their faces, an effect which the turgid state approved newsreader had never had before. Dubcek had announced it was time for Socialism with a 'human face'. There was talk of economic freedoms, even a move towards allowing other political parties over time. Censorship was re-laxed and the media became free to criticise the government. Travel restrictions were also eased. Spring that year brought real renewal. It was as if the leaves shimmering in the breeze were tiny flags of freedom, portents of a brighter tomor-row for so long denied

Stefan and Dagmar arrived early at the hotel. He nervously adjusted his tie and refused to sit down as his wife recommended.

"Where can they be? They're already twenty minutes late," he said looking at the large clock on the back wall.

"Relax, their plane was probably delayed."

Dagmar noticed a woman scanning the recep-tion. "Stefan-"

But his daughter had already spotted him and was running towards him, her stiletto heels loud on the tiled floor. They fell into each other's arms, laughing and crying at the same time.

"Klarinka, my darling Klarinka," exclaimed Stefan.

The forty-five year old woman stepped back a little. "Meet your granddaughter, Greta, and Jürgen."

Already a young woman, Greta hugged the grandfather who she had never met. Jürgen offered his hand but Stefan cast formality aside and hugged him too.

"You must be Dagmar," said Klara noticing the older woman standing to one side, beaming at this joyful reunion. "I'm happy to meet you at long last. I was so glad when I heard you and Tatka had married, so pleased to know he was no longer alone."

Stefan appreciated those words of acceptance. He'd felt awkward being there with Dagmar, so strong was his daughter's resemblance to Marta when she too had been the same age. Klara was also accomplished like her mother had been. In Germany, she'd fulfilled her dream of studying literature and now taught at the university in Munich. Her father's heart swelled with love and pride as he looked her.

Reunited with his daughter, the next few days were some of the happiest of Stefan's life. Using Deutsch Marks, his West German family treated them to meals the likes of which he hadn't eaten in years. They dined in the city's most desirable restaurants which only those with western currency or connections to those high in the Party could enter. Klara took them shopping in stores that also accepted only western currency. She insisted on buying Stefan and Dagmar new clothes despite their protestations they didn't need them and that spending time with her and her family was worth more than anything money could buy.

Part of the world's biggest refugee migration when twelve million Germans had fled or been expelled from their traditional homes in Central and Eastern Europe at the end of the war, Klara and Jürgen, like their fellow West Germans, had prospered. West Germany had risen from the ruins to become Europe's economic powerhouse, unlike Czechoslovakia whose once successful economy had fossilised under Communism.

All too soon the visit was coming to a close. "You must come visit us in Munich later in the year now things have changed. Jürgen and I will get your tickets," said Klara.

Before she left there was one place Klara asked to visit. Marta's body had never been recovered so when Pavel died, Stefan had her name added to the headstone on his son's grave. Klara and Stefan went alone. They didn't talk, each burdened by guilt. Klara for not being there for her father, he for the uncompromising line which he had taken against her for too long. Klara laid a bunch of flowers. Standing there, she reached for her father's hand and leaned her head on his shoulder.

In New York, Sara heard about the new freedoms and was seized with a sudden desire to go back to Prague. But that she was unable to do. Like during her childhood, she couldn't go outside. Sara's skin was a sickly colour and her cheeks hollow. When she walked it was as if she was a woman in her seventies not her thirties, an impression reinforced by her straggly hair streaked with grey which fell uncombed down the back of her prison uniform.

She still had several years left to serve of her sentence for robbery. The performance drugs which she had been encouraged to take in the Czechoslovak gymnastics team had made her susceptible to addiction. Soon after arriving in America, Sara had been introduced to a whole cocktail of narcotics at the parties she'd been invited to, a celebrity until she became yesterday's news.

The judge had told her that she should be ashamed, that she was fortunate to have survived the Holocaust when so few had. But he didn't understand what she had been through. How could he, she thought. The man hadn't experienced the psychological trauma which she had. Drugs were her way of forgetting, forgetting her childhood, forgetting the loss of her mother and her brother, and forgetting Edvard, who had left her not long after she became an addict.

As spring turned to summer, all of Prague

seemed to have a smile on its face. Even the way people walked had altered. The unenthusiastic shuffling of the majority who loathed Communism had given way to a brighter, more confident gait.

When in July Russian leader, Brezhnev, and his entourage arrived by train at a small Czechoslovak town to meet Dubcek, the country held its collective breath and only released it when a few days later the TV showed Brezhnev kiss Dubcek goodbye.

Tickets for the flight to Munich in September arrived.

"I can't believe we'll be going to Germany, a country I swore I'd never visit," said Stefan as he admired the bright yellow of the Lufthansa plane ticket.

"Times change. We can forever be limited by the past or we can free ourselves from it and embrace today. Who knows, maybe one day we'll even take a trip to Moscow," added Dagmar, a mischievous glint in her eye.

"No, I draw the line at that. I've already spent longer in Russia than I ever wanted to. I refuse to go back there even if I live to be a hundred."

When Stanislav turned up unexpectedly early one August morning Stefan was still dressed in his pyjamas.

CHAPTER 45

"The Russians are here," he uttered breathlessly. The colour drained from Stefan's face as the words embedded themselves. It was 1939 all over again. An overnight invasion, hopes of freedom squashed. His grandson continued: "It's time for my generation to fight for our country, like you and my father did. I'm going to make you proud of me."

"But you might be killed," objected his grandfather.

"That never stopped you. I'm going to defend the radio station, I'll be back later." He gave Stefan the briefest of hugs and tore down the stairs, naively excited at the prospect of what lay in store having never experienced the horror of combat.

Stefan woke Dagmar to give her the news. "I'm going out to see what's happening."

Quickly dressing, he made his way across town. Once more, like an alien invasion, tanks stood in line on the main thoroughfares. This time crowds of young people swarmed around them, armed with only flowers and asking the soldiers in their tanks why they had come. The soldiers had no answers for them.

On the night of 20 August, more than two hundred and fifty thousand Russians and troops from other communist countries had entered Czechoslovakia. Moscow had decided events unfolding could threaten Communism throughout the Eastern Bloc. The Czechoslovak government was asking people not to resist. In the parched heat of summer, the new life spring had ushered in was withering, and the Prague Spring, as the brief period of partial freedom had been named, was dying in plain sight.

Approaching the offices of the radio station, Stefan observed the flattened metal of trams up-ended to create a barricade which Soviet tanks had crushed with ease as they had rolled over them. One of the tanks was on fire.

An explosion rocked the air from an adjacent truck carrying ammunition, the noise echoing around the area like the loudest crack of thunder. Everybody crouched down for cover as debris flew upwards and then rained down as if metal hailstones were pounding the ground. A nearby building collapsed, and in the dust and smoke there was a cacophony of coughing. As people cautiously stood back up there followed the sound of shooting, shouts and screams coming from the direction of the radio station

A man Stefan's age stood not far from him biting the side of his index finger, agitated and anxious as he watched. A man who Stefan knew.

"Matous, what are you doing here?"

"I've come looking for my grandson. I went round to my daughter-in-law's this morning to warn her not to let him come into the city, but she said he'd already left to defend the radio station."

"Mine too is here, somewhere."

The firing ended and an eerie silence descended, bringing not peace but apprehension of what was about to be revealed. Young people appeared carrying the wounded. Stefan exhaled with relief when he saw his grandson. He was carrying, not being carried. A wail of hurt came from deep within Matous who pushed his way through the crowd to get to his grandson. The four youngsters carrying him laid him gently down. His grandfather sank to his knees and took his grandson's hand. An ambulance arrived, paramedics cramming in as many of the wounded as they could before speeding off. A man walked down the street after the vehicle waving a large Czechoslovak flag stained with blood, defiance in defeat.

Stefan went over to his grandson, his morning face of exhilaration transformed into an expression of disbelief by the force of grim reality. Stanislav's eyes reflected shattered hopes and broken dreams.

"We tried. We tried but we've failed." He was close to tears.

"No, you're heroes who faced impossible odds. You've made me very proud, and your father would be too. You should go home now, your wife and son need you."

After watching him depart, Stefan approached Matous who was staring without focus into the distance. He put his hand on Matous' shoulder. "Come, I'll go with you to the hospital."

The two old men walked dejectedly, the weight of history repeated bearing down upon them.

At the hospital Matous asked about his grandson and was told to sit, the medical staff were too busy treating those injured to come out and give updates. The two men didn't talk as they sat waiting. Each was lost in a contemplation of a life not as it should have been. Like so many, they had been the puppets of others, their destiny manipulated by strings pulled by men of evil intent. A doctor came over, her white coat smudged with crimson blotches, her solemnity cause for concern.

"Are you Miroslav Rubinsteins' grandfather." Matous nodded, unable to speak. "I'm very sorry, we were unable to save him."

When she left, Matous hung his head. Stefan reached out and held his hand of wizened skin and raised veins. It was time to stop hating the man.

A few days later Stefan and Dagmar were listening to the radio which was once more under Soviet control. Dubcek was addressing the nation, his speech punctuated with long periods of silence. They understood why, he was struggling to control his emotions. He appealed for calm, said there mustn't be provocation.

The brief promise of liberty was gone, Russian troops were here to stay and Czechoslovaks remained the Soviet Union's puppets. Not long afterwards Dubeck was out of office, sent to work in the forests.

Inside the bowels of the secret police headquarters, Stanislav was questioned. He had been picked up that morning. He didn't know the man with round glasses and penetrating eyes who was interrogating him, but the man knew of him and his family. He didn't need to check the files to know whose son the young man before him was. "The son of a traitor and now a traitor yourself," spat out the man with disgust.

Stanislav didn't rise to the bait and willed himself to stay calm. Never would he know he was talking to his family's nemesis, Yosef Rubinstein. Stanislav was released and no charges were brought but Stanislav and his wife and son were sent to live on a collective farm in the provinces. Out there, support for Communism was much stronger, and the authorities calculated that dissidents would be unlikely to meet many like minded individuals away from the major cities. In all, one hundred thousand fled into exile and half a million lost their previous jobs and any future prospects of advancement for having taken part in the uprising against the Russian invasion.

Sporadic protests continued for a while. When a student, Jan Palach, set himself alight in Wencelas Square in January 1969, two hundred thousand attended his funeral. Even more took to the streets that March when Czechoslovakia beat the Soviet Union in the finals of the world ice hockey championships, a gathering which soon turned into an anti-Russian protest. The authorities clamped down hard and all protests were forbidden.

So called 'normalisation' followed and a return to hardline Communist orthodoxy. Czechoslovakia was hypnotised by stagnation and stupor. The country became known as 'the kingdom of forgetting'. 'We pretend to work, and they pretend to pay us' was a popular saying of the era. Ever fewer believed in Communism but the state's grip had tightened. Some brave individuals, such as Vaclav Havel, spoke out against human rights abuses but they were constantly monitored and frequently imprisoned.

Stanislav was eventually allowed to return to Prague. He counted himself lucky, his experience had been nothing like his father's. Life on the collective farm had been bucolic, almost. The air was certainly fresher than in Prague and the space and greenery welcome, but being confined to the countryside was too parochial for someone raised in the capital.

Stefan was almost ninety years old when Stanislav came back. When Dagmar died, his grandson insisted he go to live with him and his wife. The stairs to the apartment where Stefan had lived all his life were becoming more than he could manage. Their apartment block had a lift he could use when it wasn't broken and awaiting repair, which was often. Their own son was married with a baby and had an apartment of his own.

It was shortly after he moved there that Stefan got word Matous, who he hadn't seen since the day at the hospital, had recently passed. Stefan missed the friend Matous had once been and Rudi also. It made him wonder sometimes what it had all been for. Maybe if there had never been the First World War and Prague had remained part of the Austro-Hungarian Empire life would have been easier. Perhaps there would have been no Nazi occupation and no Communist dictatorship. Stefan was doubtful there were many of his fellow citizens who cared about what he had sacrificed. That free and hopeful Czechoslovakia of the 1920s and 30s had become an historical footnote, forgotten it seemed by all but the old. Within another generation, no one alive would have experienced it.

The Prague Stefan loved was still visible in the distance. Those elegant spires and domes a place he no longer visited except in his dreams. He was ready to die but life wouldn't release him. Why it made him hang on he didn't understand.

Stefan lived in the past. Running around the city with Matous and Rudi, young lords of youth and laughter, ice skating on the Vltava, the thrill of meeting Dagmar as a teenager, crossing the snowy wastes of Russia on the Trans Siberian railway, the good nature and gentleness of Marta, the joy of when their children were young and they had lived as a family, those cosy Christmases, the witches' bonfires, and the puppet shows. The voices of the loved ones gone before him skipped around inside his head calling him to come join them and dance, to be free of the limits imposed by a body that ached and moved in slow motion and which tired so easily.

CHAPTER 46

"I met a friend on the way home from work," said Stanislav, himself no longer a young man and nearing fifty years of age. "He says East Germans in droves are abandoning their Trabants in the streets around the West German embassy and seeking refuge there."

His grandfather was sitting as he did every day in his armchair by the living room window so he could look down upon the people of the neighbourhood coming and going. It was something to do.

There was little on the radio or TV he cared for and the official newspaper, Rude Pravo, or Red Truth, he never read. Too much of the media was propaganda, papering over the cracks of the country's continuing decline. Instead, he found company from the puppet sitting next to him on the windowsill. It was the only one Stefan had kept when he'd moved out of his home, a young boy in a blue shirt shirt and green shorts. The wood was scratched, the paint chipped, but it was his most precious puppet. He had made it for Pavel when he was a boy. When no one was listening, Stefan would talk to the puppet. He called him Paja.

What was occurring at the West German embassy in September 1989 would prove to be an irreparable fault line in the dam of Communism. Eventually word filtered through that those concerned were to be put on trains to West Germany and freedom. Unbeknown to most in Prague massive demonstrations against the East German government followed, and in early November the Berlin Wall fell and the regime would collapse soon afterwards.

Stefan's grandson had more news for him later that month.

"People in Prague are out demonstrating in their thousands. It all started with an officially approved student demonstration to mark the fiftieth anniversary of when the Nazis brutally put down a student protest."

Stefan nodded his head. "I remember it. Your grandmother and I were glad your father hadn't gone to university or he would have been caught up in it all."

"Apparently this time it turned into a protest against the government and demands for freedom. The police trapped the crowd as they peacefully made their way in a candlelit procession to Wenceslas Square and beat them with batons. That has only served to enrage everyone. The other night over two hundred thousand gathered in Wenceslas. They're saying revolution in Poland took ten years, in Hungary ten months, in East Germany ten weeks but that we can do it in ten days. This evening there's to be a gathering on Letna Plain with even bigger crowds expected."

"I want to go."

Stanislav was taken aback. "You can't, you can barely walk."

"You can help me, and if you won't I'll crawl on my hands and knees to get there. I've been waiting a lifetime for this."

In his grandfather's milky eyes, his grandson could see a steely determination, the memories of times gone by giving him strength.

"I would help you but the lift is broken and I can't carry you down five floors."

"Go fetch Karlik. The two of you can carry me."

Something in the old man's expression stopped his grandson arguing. He had surely earned this request after all he had done and lived through. Ten minutes later, Stanislav was back with his own son. Stefan was already standing, one gnarled and arthritic hand clasped around the top of his walking stick, the other unsuccessfully trying to attach his medal to his coat, a medal which he had been obliged to hide from public view for so long.

"Let me help you." Karlik fixed it to his coat.

Stanislav and he lifted Stefan and manoeuvred him down the stairs, one holding him under the arms, the other by his lower legs.

"See, I'm not very heavy am I," the old man chuckled.

"As light as a feather."

Reaching the ground, they helped him walk to the nearby tram stop. Luckily, one was pulling in. Arriving at their destination, they began their slow walk. Stefan refused to be carried in front of so many people. Countless thousands were already there, close on a million came that night. Stanislav and Karlik carefully led Stefan nearer the stage so that despite his failing eyesight and poor hearing he would be able to witness the momentous change coming. The good natured crowd parted to let them through, some clapped and cheered to see this frail ninety-three year old joining them.

Marta Kubisova sung a song which had made her famous twenty years ago, 'A Prayer for Marta'. Her support for freedom then had abruptly ended her career. Others, including Vaclav Havel, gave speeches, ones which only days ago would have seen them arrested.

The old man gripped his grandson's arm for support. Though tears welled in his eyes, he was smiling, thinking of all those he had loved who too would have been bursting with joy at being present for this moment.

Exhausted from his exertions, Stefan didn't wake until nearly noon the following day. He reached out for the radio next to his bed, wanting confirmation that last night had been real.

Mikhail Gorbachev, the relatively youthful Russian leader, was not of the same mould as his geriatric predecessors. He had no appetite to interfere in the affairs of other countries and the Russian troops remained in their barracks.

By the end of the year, the country had its first non-majority Communist government in over forty years with the former dissident, Vaclav Havel, as President, a role he kept when his party won the democratic elections in June 1990.

The day after the election results were announced, Stanislav found his grandfather in bed in a never ending sleep. He couldn't help but think the old man had planned it this way, holding on just long enough to see his beloved homeland finally free once more.

They buried Stefan next to his son, Pavel, and Dagmar. At the end of the ceremony by the graveside, Stanislav offered his grandfather's medal to his aunt.

"You should have this. Apart from family photographs, this was his most treasured possession."

"That is sweet of you," said Klara, "but I think he would have preferred you to keep it here in Prague. It's important that it be passed to your son and his children, together with the story of your grandfather and your father, and indeed your own story, so that future generations who didn't live through the times we did never take their freedom for granted. If too many of us in Europe forget our past, then history will repeat itself. Freedom is fragile and easily trampled. Twice this century we've seen that happen in this country. Only by keeping the past alive can that we stop it from happening again. It's also the best way in which we can honour the memory of my parents and your father, and all the others who gave their lives for us to be free."

As they stood there a sound began, a sonorous sound which was timeless. At first, there was only a solitary one. Soon many others joined. It made them both smile. The bells of Prague were chiming.

+++

ALSO BY DAVID CANFORD

A Good Nazi? The Lies We Keep

Growing up in 1930s Germany two boys, one Catholic and one Jewish, become close friends. After Hitler seizes power, their lives are changed forever. When World War 2 comes, will they help each other, or will secrets from their teenage years make them enemies?

Kurt's War

Kurt is an English evacuee with a difference. His father is a Nazi. As Kurt grows into an adult and is forced to pretend that he is someone he isn't for his own protection, will he survive in the hostile world in which he must live? And with his enemies closing in, will even the woman he loves believe who he really is?

Going Big or Small

British humour collides with European culture in this tale of 'it's never too late'. Retiree, Frank, gets more adventure than he bargained for when he sets off across 1980s Europe hoping to shake up his mundane life. Falling in love with a woman and Italy has unexpected consequences.

Betrayal in Venice

Sent to Venice on a secret mission against the Nazis, a soldier finds his life unexpectedly altered when he saves a young woman at the end of World War Two. Discovering the truth many years later, Glen Butler's reaction to it betrays the one he loves most.

The Throwback

A baby's birth on a South Carolina plantation threatens to cause a scandal, but the funeral of mother and child seems to ensure that the truth will never be known. A family saga of hatred, revenge, forbidden love, overcoming hardship and helping others.

Sweet Bitter Freedom

The sequel to the Throwback. Though the Civil

War has now ended, Mosa is confronted by new challenges and old adversaries who are determined to try and take what she has. While some hope to build a new South, the old South refuses to die. Will Mosa lose everything or find a way through?

A Heart Left Behind

New Yorker, Orla, finds herself trapped in a web of secret love, blackmail and espionage in the build up to WW2. Moving to Berlin and hoping to escape her past, she is forced to undertake a task that will cost not only her own life but also that of her son if she fails.

Bound Bayou

A young teacher from England achieves a dream when he gets the chance to work for a year in the United States, but 1950s Mississippi is not the America he has seen on the movie screens at home. When his independent spirit collides with the rules of life in the Deep South, he sets off a chain of events he can't control.

Sea Snakes and Cannibals

A travelogue of visits to islands around the world, including remote Fijan islands, Corsica, islands in the Sea of Cortez, Mexico, and the Greek islands.

When the Water Runs out

Will water shortage result in the USA invading Canada? One person can stop a war if he isn't killed first but is he a hero or a traitor? When two very different worlds collide, the outcome is on a knife-edge.

2045 The Last Resort
In 2045 those who lost their jobs to robots are taken care of in resorts where life is an endless vacation. For those still in work, the American dream has never been better. But is all quite as perfect as it seems?

SIGN UP

Don't forget to sign up at DavidCanford.com to receive David Canford's email newsletter including information on new releases and promotions and claim your free ebook.

THANK YOU

I hope you enjoyed reading Puppets of Prague. I would appreciate it if you could spare a few moments to post a review on Amazon. It only need be a few words.

Thanks so much,

David Canford
ABOUT THE AUTHOR

David started writing stories for his grandmother as a young boy. They usually involved someone being eaten by a monster of the deep, with his grandmother often the hapless victim.

Years later as chair lady of her local Women's Institute, David's account of spending three days on a Greyhound bus crossing the United States from the west coast to the east coast apparently saved the day when the speaker she had booked didn't show up.

David's life got busy after university and he stopped writing until the bug got him again recently.

As an indie author himself, David likes discovering the wealth of great talent which is now so easily accessible. A keen traveller, he can find a book on travel particularly hard to resist.

He enjoys writing about both the past and what might happen to us in the future.

Cambridge University educated, his previous jobs include working as a mover in Canada and a sandblaster in the Rolls Royce aircraft engine factory. David works as a lawyer during the day. He has three daughters and lives on the south coast of England with his wife and their dog.

A lover of both the great outdoors and the man-made world, he is equally happy kayaking, hiking a trail or wandering around a city absorbing its culture.

You can contact him by visiting his website at DavidCanford.com

Printed in Great Britain
by Amazon